HUBRIS FALLS

FRIENDSHIP
RLISY HEROISM DRUGS IMMEDIAC
LICANS SANCTITY LOYALTY COU
INTOLERANCE HIGH TURMOIL DIS
RITUALITY DISAFFECTED TURBUL
MPTION DEATH ACCEPTANCE LUDI
ATEFUL FALLING ROCK N ROLL TH
HTING QUESTIONS ALCOHOL POLIT
NVERGING PHILOSOPHY MUSHROO
REASONABLE LIFE YOUTH ISOLAT
URAGE WEED DEFIANCE EVOLUTIO
RSEVERANCE DEPRESSION DELUSI
NATURAL SELECTION LAUGHTER
FAIR ORDEAL DETERMINATION DA
ADVENTURE IGNORANCE MIND AU
RANCE JUDGEMENT UNEASE N
ATED MAGNIFICENT ANTICS
CONFORMITY HONOR

HUBRIS FALLS

a novel

Matthew S. Hiley

GREENLEAF
BOOK GROUP PRESS

Published by Greenleaf Book Group Press
Austin, Texas
www.gbgpress.com

Distributed by Greenleaf Book Group

For ordering information or special discounts for bulk purchases, please contact Greenleaf Book Group at PO Box 91869, Austin, TX 78709, 512.891.6100.

Design and composition by Greenleaf Book Group
Cover design by Greenleaf Book Group and Brian Phillips

Previously published in 2010 by Matthew Hiley
(ISBN: 978-0615377780).

Publisher's Cataloging-in-Publication data is available.

Print ISBN: 978-1-62634-649-9

eBook ISBN: 978-1-62634-650-5

Part of the Tree Neutral® program, which offsets the number of trees consumed in the production and printing of this book by taking proactive steps, such as planting trees in direct proportion to the number of trees used: www.treeneutral.com

Printed in the United States of America on acid-free paper

19 20 21 22 23 24 25   10 9 8 7 6 5 4 3 2 1

Second Edition

For the legions of teachers who inspire their students to think for themselves and follow their dreams . . .

For Chris Devero, my hetero life partner and wingman, taken far too soon, who showed us all how to live . . .

For Graham King, who carved a path in our spirits that will never be forgotten . . .

For JB Paisley, Derrick Hamilton, Jimmy Smith Jr., and Ryan Williams . . . Do they make friends any better?

For my father, Randy; my mother, Vickie; and my brother, Jason, whose unending support made this possible . . .

And mostly . . .

For the love of a lifetime, my wife, Gretchen, and my children, Emma, Ella, Violette, and Holden . . . you help me find the beauty in life every single day.

hubris /hyoo-brĭs/

> *n.*: Overbearing pride or arrogance of presumed knowledge

fall /fôl/

> *v.*: **1.** To drop or descend under the force of gravity **2.** To become less or lower; become of a lower level *n.*: **1.** A succumbing to temptation **2.** A cataract or waterfall

PROLOGUE

02/21/06

S hit. The weight of life is just bearing down on me so hard right now. I don't know what to do.

I found sobriety for the first time in my life not too long ago, and already I feel as if I'm going to lose it. I feel like I can't hang on to it. It's slipping away, and I'm losing my grip.

And I don't want it to go away. I like it. But the world is just so fucked. I thought sobriety would make the world seem better, but I'm starting to rethink the comfort of the numbness I've called home for so long.

This planet is so wild now, so alive—and so ready to kill itself. I am in awe of it.

But whether or not I am a part of it, it seems headed for destruction. The whole scale of things is just so out of whack—from the big picture to my little picture, globally and locally, physically and mentally *fucked*.

I feel like I've survived outside it all for so long. I look at everything now and wonder, *How have we arrived here? How have I arrived here?*

The world, our country, other countries, politics, religion, fanaticism, unilateralism, fundamentalism, society, immunity, community, family, war, destruction, desolation, famine, poverty, flooding, hurricanes, mining, right-wing, left-wing, progressive, regressive, monogamous, lobotomous . . . It's all fucked.

And I've wanted to tell my story for so long, but I wanted to tell it with a happy ending. I keep waiting for it. That bastard of a happy ending keeps delaying itself, but the story needs to be told.

Not because of some grandiose idea I have of myself or of my experiences but because, as I look at my story through these eyes of sobriety, I see that it runs parallel to all of this crazy, stupid shit we have come to call our existence.

I've got to see whether I can make sense of it—whether anyone can.

What's wrong with this place? Why do we keep making the same mistakes over and over? Why can't we just learn for once? Why do we shed our innocence so early on and become raging assholes intent on destroying ourselves and others for temporary artificial happiness?

We grow up being spoon-fed things: which God to worship, which party to vote for, what color people we should trust. And then, sometimes, something happens that turns all of that shit on its head. Then we have a whole new outlook on things.

But we have to reconcile when that happens.

"Okay, in light of this life-altering event that has just occurred, what parts of my old life are now acceptable?"

What do we trust at that point? Once someone pulls back the curtains and shows you the strings, it's hard to look at those damn puppets the same.

It's just like Santa Claus. One day, you find out he's not real. We are actually celebrating Jesus's birthday. "Sorry about the trick! And there are no elves, just midgets." But then everybody has a different take on Jesus. "He's got a great message of peace. So if those fuckers over there won't believe in him, kill them all." Oh, okay.

Jesus died two thousand years ago, yet all of these people who've never met him are suddenly able to give his opinion on everything. "Yeah, I know he was all about love. But he hated gay people. Gay people will turn your kids gay, and then your kids will go to Hell with all of the other gay people."

Right. Jesus totally said that. He said it in a megachurch in Nazareth—right after he spoke of the duty of good Christians to deplete the Earth of its resources and ignore people who are less fortunate and in need of assistance.

So where the hell am I going with this? And how in holy fuck have I already talked about sobriety, depression, Christmas, hurricanes, Jesus, and gay people in so few pages?

I keep thinking about this rafting trip I took after I graduated from college. It was one of those events that forced my life down a completely different avenue. Since that trip, I haven't been able to get my shit together at all. Like the girl who works the VIP room at a strip joint, I have unresolved issues.

That trip my friends and I took was nine years ago. For nine years, I've carried this weight. It was to the Rio Grande, which traverses the southernmost edge of these United States. And on that trip, on that river, all of the most wonderful and horrible things we see represented in this world—in this life—came crashing together in a most fantastic tragedy.

As lives hung in the balance, the idealism and cynicism and invincibility of youth converged, forcing me and my friends to confront who we were.

The trip was supposed to take five days. But when you're twenty-three years old and wild at heart, a five-day trip should never take five days. It should take four or less because you have gone balls to the wall in your gusto for life and excitement, because going too fast is one of life's great gifts, or it should take six or greater because you have spent too much time smoking that fine homegrown basement ganja and waxing philosophic on the great trials and tribulations of man. Either way, if a five-day trip takes five days, something has gone horribly wrong.

And we all know this by now: *Shit happens.*

That's just life, as they say. And what a tortured thing it can be. Even the easy life can be difficult, if you dwell on it. Why *are* there so many songs about rainbows? And what *is* on the other side? Nothing. Nothing but air. Rainbows are just illusions. That's it.

At a young age, we seem to have a good grip on this. Yet as we get longer and longer in the tooth, we try harder and harder to make that fucking rainbow *real*.

We knew as kids that the rainbow wasn't real. They showed us in science class how it all worked. It was a refraction of light, bending it through this condensation prism we could almost comprehend. It usually followed shitty weather, or perhaps preceded it. It meant nothing. It achieved nothing. It was just there. And we loved rainbows.

Being young is when everything has meaning, and that meaning is that nothing means anything. Nothing is of value other than being able to live and breathe free and feel *this* moment. Tomorrow is a concept that can't be processed; it can't be breached.

I don't want to get into all of the psychobabble bullshit about carpe diem; that's dated. Nobody at a young age wants to seize the day. They want to seize the *right fucking now*.

That was all we wanted to do. That's why I don't feel we deserved what we got in return. We just wanted to seize the now.

This moment. Right now. Pass the joint. Right now. Gimme some shroomies, baby. Right now. Pass me sixteen ounces of cold, stinky, $9.99-for-a-thirty-pack beer. Right now.

Was this the right attitude to have back then? An easy argument could be made either way. It might be an easy argument for any age. But I'm not trying to build a case. I'm trying to figure shit out.

Maybe I just want the rainbow to be real now, regardless of what is true. But I just have to tell this to get past it.

I kept a journal in those days and wrote in it almost every night. I put it all together right after it happened. It's been sitting there ever since, waiting for, as I said, a happy ending—a "movie of the week" ending. But now I just want an ending.

I put it on the shelf years ago. And I've been hiding from myself ever since—still trying to seize the now, but with anger. And with diminishing returns.

I had such a great group of friends back then. Anyone would be lucky to have friends so good. It started so well to end so badly.

So here it is. Forgive me. We were just kids, you know?

FRIENDSHIP HATE M
POCRISY HEROISM DRUGS IMMOR
RICANS SANCTITY LOYALTY COW
T INTOLERANCE HIGH TURMOIL D
RITUALITY DISAFFECTED TURBU
MPTION DEATH ACCEPTANCE LUD
ATEFUL FALLING ROCK 'N ROLL T
GHTING QUESTIONS ALCOHOL POLI
ONVERGING PHILOSOPHY MUSHRO
NREASONABLE LIFE YOUTH ISOLA
URAGE WEED DEFIANCE EVOLUTI
RSEVERANCE DEPRESSION DELUS
NATURAL SELECTION LAUGHTER
FAIR ORDEAL DETERMINATION D
ADVENTURE IGNORANCE MIND A
RIENCE JUDGEMENT UNEASE N
BATED MAGNIFICENT ANTIC
CONFORMITY HONOR

PART I
Greased Enlightening

1

05/17/97

Holy shit. My friends and I graduated from college today. Amazing. What a sad statement that is for our educational system.

The great Albert Einstein once said, "Education is that which remains when one has forgotten everything he learned in school."

Okay, Albert. I believe that makes me educated.

During the graduation ceremony, we listened to various professors and deans hand out awards that we never even knew existed. Not that we would have been in contention, mind you, but maybe it would have been nice to know five years ago, when I began my college life, that there were awards to be handed out upon graduation.

I wanted to be happy for the fine scholars who received those awards while we watched, but I found it difficult. These were the very same folks who always fucked up the curve. And now they were being rewarded for it? It was hard to stomach. I was glad I was wasted.

Ironically, one of these award winners had turned Jimmy and me in during our sophomore year for drinking in the dorms. He was just a douchebag freshman then. Maybe he was justified.

The guy had lived in the room below us and had his TV and VCR on the window ledge to get maximum reception. And when Jimmy threw up out of the window upstairs, he couldn't have known he would be dousing this guy's entertainment zone in vomit . . . while the guy was sitting there playing video games.

If I remembered the incident correctly, however, he didn't actually turn us in the night that Jimmy drenched his entertainment system. It was the next night, when Jimmy and I came back drunk again, and Jimmy threw up again, and this time, the guy had his laundry on his window ledge.

I would've been more pissed about the TV and VCR, but I guess he really liked that shirt.

I still couldn't remember the guy's name, even though I'd met him a thousand times. Hell, they even mentioned his name twice from the stage, but I was way too drunk to pick up on it.

Also, we hadn't gone to sleep the previous night. Instead, we had all sat around discussing whether there were codes in the Bible that foretold the future, just like in that bestselling book that came out that year.

Folks have been looking to ancient documents to foresee the future for many moons. There have been many interesting discoveries—all of which are based on such randomness that it appears as if, with much investigation and sliding of numbers and rearranging of words, you could tell the future from any book in the world. And what better way to sell books than apocalyptic, fear-mongering bullshit?

It usually took a five-foot bong to provoke such a discussion, and this time was no different. We had also been drinking since noon.

We soon realized that our current topic was a new low in the realm of deep thinking. We switched to arguing about Plato and Aristotle, which soon became horribly uninteresting, due in large part to our limited knowledge. After that, it was politics, so we all got a chance to yell. Really, we were just savoring the moment. This would be one of our last great all-night debates.

We didn't want to own up to that fact that everything was all gonna be over soon, but it weighed heavily on our minds as we continued drinking and passing the peace pipe.

Right around midnight, Jimmy, my closest friend, informed me that he did not believe that in our five years of higher education I had ever outdrank him. I disagreed. Because I disagreed, Jimmy and I were still engaged in a drinking contest during our graduation. Now, an outsider might've thought that Jimmy would have had the edge on me in a drinking contest. But that's why such a person would be referred to as an outsider.

Jimmy stood about six foot, three inches tall. He was a huge mountain of muscle. He weighed in at around 230 pounds. I was six feet tall but somewhere in the neighborhood of half of Jimmy's weight, with pretty much zero muscle. But I had an uncanny knack for being an underdog success.

(I didn't, really—but I could bullshit myself quite well.)

As we sat there watching the great accomplishment that was a college education coming to a head, we couldn't help but glance across the auditorium occasionally at each other to make sure we were both still in the contest, as it had become increasingly obvious that it would soon end.

It was an unfortunate circumstance that graduation from college had to interfere with such a monumental task as a true man-to-man drinking contest.

I'm quite sure that everyone I had encountered that day was aware that I was involved in a drinking contest.

I'm *not* quite sure, though, that it was pride I saw gleaming in my father's eye when I told him loudly over lunch with my extended family just before the ceremony what we were up to. "Goddammit! I'm gonna win!" I told him with enthusiasm.

But there we were. Jimmy and I each had a flask that was to be emptied during the diplomathon.

At some point the next day, we were supposed to be leaving for a backpacking and rafting adventure to Big Bend National Park, in South Texas, where we would be hiking through the Monahan Sand Dunes to the glorious Rio Grande River, where we would then be rafting for five days along the southern border of the United States of America.

We had been looking forward to this trip for weeks.

It was the last thing I remember thinking about before I blacked out.

2

"**O**h my god, Becky, look at her butt. It's so big."

That's what I was waking up to: "Baby Got Back" by Sir Mix-a-Lot was playing extremely loudly as I tried to get my bearings.

I was hoping not only that I was regaining consciousness in the comfort of my own apartment—which, often enough, wasn't the case—but also that the large black man on my floor beside me was Jimmy.

Had I taken a lover? I reached around to make sure my ass was still intact and hadn't been violated. Then Jim rolled over enough for me to recognize him, and I breathed a sigh of relief.

I looked around. My entire flight crew was present and accounted for.

JB was packing a bong. JB was great at packing bongs. He almost appeared to be made for it by some form of intelligent design. He had a short torso and short legs. Hell, I guess that made him short. But he had ridiculously long arms. I guess he was built like a slender silverback ape, but he wasn't really slender; only if he actually were an ape would you say that. And his short torso put him in close proximity to the bowl portion of the bong. He could grab a bag of weed halfway across the room with his long-ass arms while never leaving the airspace of the bong. Amazing. As an added benefit, there was never much risk of his stubby little legs knocking over a floor-kept bong.

Williams was pouring what appeared to be a Jack and Coke, hold the Coke. Williams was the guy you think of as an asshole character in a movie like *Pretty in Pink* or *The Karate Kid*. He wasn't the main asshole but the asshole's less attractive buddy. Williams had always been portly (read: fat) and had started losing the thin, dark hair on his head and getting it on his face at around age twelve. When he wore a hat (which was always), he looked to be about our age. When he took the hat off, he looked forty-five. None of the hair regrowth shit ever worked for him. This is why he drank whiskey in the morning and looked like an asshole. He came from a very wealthy family, though, so he was always of the opinion that he looked pretty fucking good to the ladies. He did not.

Devero, my dark-skinned buddy of unknown ethnicity, was arranging what looked like equal portions of the caps and stems from a bag of psychedelic mushrooms. We could never figure Devero out. His parents were both pasty white, yet he was pretty dark. He looked white. He had white features. He was just unexplainably dark, almost brown. He claimed he wasn't adopted. He had dark, straight white-guy hair and a white-guy nose. Just strange. You've gotta think his mom might have thrown a leg up to a Pakistani on the side—or a Cuban. Who knows?

Anyway, that was all of us. Jimmy, JB, Devero, Williams, and me.

"Nice job yesterday, Legs," said Devero while attempting a breakdancing move.

I stretched my mind back, but I couldn't remember anything past the graduation ceremony.

"Legs" was a nickname of mine for my outstanding achievements in foosball. I had the best defensive leg in the league—assuming there was a league.

"Where are my parents?" I asked.

"They caught an early flight home yesterday," Devero said. "After you fell down walking toward the stage and passed out, I think they might've been embarrassed."

"Shit."

"When you finally got up, I actually thought they might stay. Then you threw up everywhere, and the janitors had to clean up the aisle so people could continue to walk down it. Some students had to leave and not get their diplomas because of the smell, so your folks left." He smirked at me.

"They told me to tell you how proud they were. You won the drinking contest."

"I did? You sure?"

"By the time you passed out, Jimmy had been snoring for ten minutes."

I knew that Devero enjoyed the fact that my parents liked him the best of all my friends. I think they liked him out of sympathy for his mom's obvious infidelity, although I held that opinion close to the vest.

"Well," I said, "it may have been poor timing. In fact, I'm sure of it. But Jimmy had to be put in his place. You just don't call a man out like that, especially not while in a debate on the complexities of the human condition."

"A man's gotta do what a man's gotta do," Devero replied. "No one here questions your integrity."

"By the way," I asked, "did a cat shit in my mouth, or is that my breath?"

"Doesn't really matter. Either way, it's your breath," Devero said.

I sat up and gazed around the shitty apartment that I shared with Jimmy. It was amazing that I could even smell my own breath. The fucking place sucked. It was disgusting, with spittoon beer cans all over the place. It was a dimly lit, depressing, unhygienic, shag-carpeted slum.

There were two bedrooms, each of which stank to high heaven, and a bathroom that made the bedrooms smell like a florist's shop. The kitchen and living room were barely discernable from one another; the eight-foot stretch of thirty-year-old linoleum was the only signal that you had entered the kitchen.

The ceiling fan in the living room was down to one blade. It had been a four-blade fan originally, but in our defense, it only had three when we moved in. One blade was lost when Devero decided to prove to us that ceiling fans were so safe these days that you could literally stop one with your head. It cost him five stitches in the emergency room, and he still has no memory of that entire week. The other blade was due to that asshole Williams, who simply *had* to know the answer to that age-old question: What would happen if you threw a cat into a ceiling fan? The cat was fine, and we ended up beating Williams's ass for being such a dick, but it still cost us a fan blade. We also whacked Williams in the face with that very fan blade when he passed out that night.

So, yup, my place sucked. But it was our castle, and we loved it unconditionally.

I quickly discovered that unlike everybody else (including Jimmy), I had not received my diploma. It also appeared, through word of my faithful band of brothers, that upon leaving the ceremony while being propped up by campus security, I had become aware that I had parked my car illegally. Due to multiple security/parking issues with which I had been associated, my vehicle was at this time being towed.

This was because of the school's "tow list." Once a student reached a certain number of unpaid traffic or security violations within a given amount of time, their vehicle was placed on the tow list until all fines were paid. But I wasn't supposed to be on the tow list anymore, because I had paid the fines to clear my record only the day before. I was told that I had to do this in order to get my diploma, but here I was being towed nonetheless. That must have been why seeing the tow truck had pissed me off so fucking much. Possibly I had reacted a tad irrationally. I don't remember.

Apparently, as I was being escorted from the auditorium, I had tried to politely let these fine security personnel know that I was off the tow list, but they wouldn't listen. So I offered some opinions, things got heated; I paid the tow truck guy, and I left. Shitfaced.

It now appeared that if I wanted my diploma, I had to visit the dean of students, Lawrence Horton, a man who was not a day less than ninety by the looks of him.

It was explained to me that he would dole out my final punishment at this fine institution for yesterday's events—of which I had little recollection. One last damn thing and then we could all pack up and leave.

Ever the genius, I made my trek after partaking in some hair of the dog—my old friend Jack Daniel's—and a large hit from the hookah. Then I made my way over to the dean's office to clear this whole misunderstanding up.

As Dean Horton welcomed me grimly into his office, I began thinking that perhaps the hookah had been the wrong instrument to bring me into these settings. And assuming that was true, the Jack had been just plain ludicrous.

The dean's office was large and prestigious. Recognitions of shit this guy had accomplished in the last 197 years were hung along every inch of his walls. His desk was equally large and prestigious. Was he compensating for something? Maybe not: Maybe the guy was hiding a huge elderly penis under that desk.

All I knew was that he looked three feet tall behind that thing. He had huge ears, too—almost alarmingly huge, like Yoda. But he had the voice of Darth Vader, and he commanded respect.

Dean Horton asked me to recount what I thought the events of the day before had been.

In the spirit of candor, I provided him with a very factual account of the events that had occurred as I recollected them, with absolutely no variation from the truth whatsoever.

"Well," I began, "I had been pretty nervous leading up to graduation. It's a pretty major event in any person's life. And finals were really tough on me this time. I was taking some difficult classes, and I was so nervous the night before graduation that I didn't sleep.

"So when my name was called to retrieve my diploma from the stage, it all just kind of came down on me. The pressure was intense, you know? I collapsed. And I was so nervous, and maybe some food disagreed with me; my seafood smelled really fishy last night—not fishy like suspicious, but maybe. But more likely fishy because it wasn't fresh. And I think it all just kind of hit me at once, and I threw up."

I shook my head.

"I'm real sorry about that," I said, with a combination of cockiness and sheepishness.

I paused to hit him with an appropriately contrite look before barreling on. "Anyhow, as I was being led outside for a breath of fresh air, I noticed my vehicle was being towed, even though I was supposed to be off the tow list. After a brief discussion, the security officers and the tow truck guy let me have my car and leave."

"So that's what happened?" asked the distinguished old gent.

"Yes, sir," I replied. "That's about it." I was gaining that confidence you get when you almost start to believe yourself.

"Would you mind if I read to you what the head of security on the scene, one of the gentlemen who escorted you out and helped with the tow truck incident, had to say?"

"Not at all, sir," I replied, although I didn't particularly like where this could potentially head.

The dean looked down at an official-looking paper in his hands.

"As Mr. Hamilton stood to walk the aisle to receive his diploma, he stumbled a few feet and fell over, sprawled out in the middle of the aisle. It appeared as though he had fallen asleep.

"We tried to wake him, and he shook us off violently and stood up, telling us something about us not knowing shit about Jerry Garcia and the way the world should be. After another couple of steps, Mr. Hamilton began vomiting. He smelled overwhelmingly of alcohol, and his speech was very slurred."

Dean Horton gave me a piercing look over the tops of his glasses before returning to the security guard's statement.

"We tried to carry him outside away from the building. As we were carrying him, he kept telling us that he could see that his car was being towed and that it shouldn't be. He became belligerent.

"Then he broke free and ran toward the tow truck driver. He began poking him in the chest and cursing at him. He called him a 'stupid motherfucker' multiple times."

My god, it was priceless hearing the dean say that.

"Then," the dean continued, "we pulled Mr. Hamilton back. He was obviously drunk, but we checked the list, and we actually did confirm that he had paid his fines. As the tow truck driver was unloading the vehicle, Mr. Hamilton walked up to him and got less than an inch from his nose and yelled 'Ha!,' clearly startling the man, so we decided to calm Mr. Hamilton down and write him a disorderly conduct ticket."

The dean cleared his throat juicily before continuing. The phlegm in his throat popped around like lottery balls.

"As I was informing him of his offense," he read, "he told me to 'go fuck myself' and sprinted to his car, where he immediately locked himself in. As we tried to tell him to roll down his window, he made faces with his hand to his ear, pretending he couldn't hear us, and then he drove away. Then he stopped, came back a short distance from us, climbed halfway out of his sunroof, extended the middle fingers of both hands, and told us to 'suck his balls.'"

The dean set down the guard's statement and just stared at me for a few moments before continuing.

"I am paraphrasing and rounding out our security guard's statement, but he does quote you verbatim. Now tell me, Mr. Hamilton, does that sound like a more accurate account of events?"

Of course I said no and stuck to my guns about having a nervous stomach, even though at that very moment I was well over half-cocked from the Jack and ganja. The dean stuck to his guns too and told me that I must pay my disorderly conduct fine and write a letter of apology to the tow truck driver and the security officers in order to receive my diploma.

Big deal. I began to make a mental note about not telling security officers to suck my balls after winning a drinking contest. And driving. But I was interrupted in thought. He wasn't done.

"Brian, I know that inside of you lies a very intelligent person. But you're too interested in making life difficult for authority figures."

This was not true. I made life difficult for a very diverse group of people. I held no particular prejudice against authority figures. In fact, often the authority figures were just collateral damage.

And I knew that somewhere deep down inside this old windbag was probably someone who was *also* intelligent. He just happened to be in the wrong place at the wrong time, as dean. It often seemed in these meetings that he actually did care, though, and did want to see me make good of myself. Hell, I was glad for what I did just because I got to see this old guy again. I would sorely miss him.

"Well, sir, I'll make sure I get those letters of apology out right away. I wouldn't want those gentlemen getting the wrong impression about my intentions. And no disrespect to you, sir, but I must be going now. I have a great summer trip planned, and we leave today."

He stood up to walk me to the door, placing a hand on my shoulder. Once at the door, he stopped and turned toward me. He extended his arm to shake my hand. When our hands were clasped together, he gripped tightly and pulled me in close.

"You take care of yourself, Brian. You are capable of so much, son. Be *good*. Don't stare into the abyss too long; sometimes it stares back."

4

It was beginning to get a bit late, almost four. My little meeting with Dean Horton had set us back. People kept calling me, and I had to keep telling the story to them. And then, of course, I had to talk to my parents.

I had begun to believe that my father felt as though he had been far too lenient with his children. It's okay when you pull a prank and your parents grudgingly laugh. Hell, that's great. It's as if they've momentarily seen you as an equal.

But when you fall down, pass out, and throw up in the aisle at your college graduation ceremony, they don't laugh. What you get instead is that worst possible reaction: disappointment. It was overwhelming in my father's voice when I finally had the balls to call him.

I could tell he was becoming less and less sure of letting me enter into the family business—and rightfully so. I didn't know dick about real estate, although my new degrees said otherwise. And it isn't as if real estate was even what I wanted to do. But we talked it out, and they seemed relieved that I would be getting my diploma after all. College was over. I had probably not made them proud, but I had graduated and they grudgingly had to respect that.

We finally got on the road as night began to fall. JB's father was a car dealer in the area, and we were able to coax him into lending us a custom full-sized van for the ride, complete with a TV, VCR, video game system, and refrigerator. It was a shame that the fine folks at the van company didn't market such vans to youthful demographics. I couldn't imagine a vehicle more suited to my generation.

To start the road trip out right, Jimmy had rolled a joint. And to be quite fair, to call this thing he'd created a "joint" would be comparable to calling Hezbollah a faith-based organization. It was roughly the size of a guitar neck. Jimmy applied flame to the end, and before long, the cabin of the van was filled with smoke so thick you could spread it on bread.

Driving intoxicated is dangerous, irresponsible, and a disgusting act to commit upon your fellow citizens. Having said that, I can't recall a road trip I've ever been on where everyone in the car wasn't trashed. I mean, don't get me wrong; the driver was usually in better shape than the others, but still.

JB was driving. After the initial rush wore off, I was the first one to realize that we were moving less than twenty miles per hour on the interstate; we weren't so much driving as we were a portrait of mass in motion. At this rate, the twelve-hour drive to the Monahan Sand Dunes might take close to three days. Something had to be done.

"Hey, dicknose," I called out to JB.

Silence followed. It must have been unclear which dicknose I was addressing.

"Hey, JB," I tried again.

"What's up, dicknose?" he replied.

"You do realize that we were late getting started, that we're all higher than ninjas, and that we're going nineteen in a sixty-five, right?"

"Nineteen? Man, I'm high. I thought I was going seventy-nine."

"Not unless all of those cars passing us are doing one-thirty."

"You may be right."

"Yeah, I mean, it's good to be safe, but . . ."

"Point taken. I can't see straight, so stop fucking with me. I need to concentrate."

And concentrate he did. I don't know what kind of Jedi-like state he entered after that, but I don't believe we heard from JB for a good three hours.

He didn't say a word until the dog hit the windshield. None of us saw it coming. It was spectacular.

We had picked up speed considerably as the night got thick. We had been following a Trans Am with "AC/DC" and "No Fear" bumper stickers, displaying the character of the character inside. The windows were tinted, but it was easy to imagine what type of guy was behind the wheel: well-groomed mullet, thin and barely discernable mustache.

Our speedometer was clocking well past eighty-five and was pinned back at zero, where that little thing sticks out to stop that other thing from going around again. The steady speed had put us in a stupor, but we were all jolted from our reverie by a loud *wham!* on the hood and then again on the front window.

"Dude! What the hell did you just hit?" screamed Devero.

"Dude! You killed somebody!" yelled Jimmy.

"Just keep goin', man!" added Williams.

"It wasn't a person, guys," JB said after a long monastic level of silence. "I think it was a dog. Whatever the hell it was, part of it is stuck on the hood. I think it's a dog arm. Or leg. It's waving at us. It wasn't us that hit the dog, though. It exploded on that Trans Am in front of us. That bastard isn't even pulling over . . . In fact, he's speeding up! What kind of world do we live in?"

We all sat in stunned silence as we drove. We were in shock.

Every few moments, a little chunk of carcass would flop up onto the window and slowly slide upward until it disappeared over the roof. Whenever that happened, we would all look up in unison to the sunroof to watch it pass.

We finally remembered to turn the windshield wipers on. Slowly, the smears of blood cleared. The leg was still waving from where it was stuck in the hood.

We would occasionally wave back.

There was no point in stopping to see if the dog was okay. The evidence spoke for itself. He was obviously waving from the afterlife.

"You know, guys," said Jimmy, "I'm not happy to see a dog go down. It's a sad thing, no doubt. But if the shit's gonna happen, I'd rather be there than not."

We cracked a few more beers. It was one of those great moments in life where you just feel good with your friends. Your *true* friends. We were living our lives without a care in the world. No jobs. No responsibility. Just right now, this moment. Road trip . . . Was there *ever* anything better?

5

It was good to see Jimmy getting back to having fun. His father and his only sibling—his fourteen-year-old brother Darrell—had been killed in a car accident last summer. Since the accident, we had all been doing everything we could to make sure Jimmy was okay. We had all feared his father and loved his brother.

Jimmy was the black sheep of our flock—literally. He was black. The rest of us were stone-cold honkies—although Devero did look oddly Mexican. Or Iraqi. But we've covered that.

This meant we had always had a front row seat to racism happening all around us. Anyone who says it doesn't exist anymore must not have any black friends. And sometimes even those who had black friends were racist. I had even been a little racist myself sometimes.

Jimmy got thrown in detention with Devero and me in the eighth grade. Devero and I were there for pinning our dissected frogs to the message board at the school entrance in a provocative position. Jimmy was in for stealing all of the athletic tape from the supply closet in the locker room and then taping the door to the coach's office shut while the coach was still inside. He had used *a lot* of tape. The coach had been inside for eight hours or so when the cleaning crew finally heard him banging on the door.

Naturally, we admired Jimmy instantly. He fit right in to our group of misfits. Ignorant black kids called him a sellout because most of his friends were white, and ignorant white kids called him worse names because he was black. It wasn't as big an issue with our "enlightened" age group as it might have been in earlier generations, but it was all undeniably still there.

Last June, Jimmy's father and Darrell had been heading back from a baseball game when bad luck was compounded with bad luck. And an extra helping of bad luck was thrown in for the sake of absurdity.

Jimmy's dad, James Sr., was driving his new Mazda at three miles per hour over the speed limit, with Darrell in the passenger seat. As he was passing through an intersection, his vehicle was T-boned on the passenger side by a twenty-year-old Chevy truck doing twice the speed limit. Darrell was killed instantly, and James Sr. died moments later of internal injuries, cradling Darrell in his lap.

This is where the bad luck got worse. The driver of the truck was a lifelong criminal, repeatedly let out of prison too early, who had just robbed a convenience store before he ran the red light and killed half of Jimmy's family. He had "white power" prison tattoos all over his body. Confederate flags adorned his truck's rear window, with the motto "The South Will Rise Again." It was just like a bad made-for-TV movie. But I guess that shit on TV actually happens sometimes.

At the sentencing, when the judge asked if this bastard had any regrets, he grinned as he replied, "Only that those two niggers got in my way."

The comment made national news, meaning that, for months,

Jimmy and his mother had to deal with blood-sucking reporters angling for journalistic fame, ringing the doorbell and asking, "So, how do you feel?"

During the past year, Jimmy had become more and more involved in his church. He had always been religious, which had always been a source of tension between us, especially as I turned more and more away from God. He was constantly trying to repackage and resell Jesus to me, and my rejection only made his faith stronger. It shocked me to no end how someone could go through so much without having his faith the least bit shaken. Jimmy even wrote the bastard letters in prison on a regular basis, telling him he had forgiven him for his actions and for his words. The letters came back unopened.

6

Okay, so we were in the middle of our last free summer. Free rent. Free spirits. Free beer.

Our summer was free because we were in that wonderful spot between diploma and job. Our rent was free because our parents had mercy on our collective unemployed hobo status. Our spirits were free because that's what the road does to you. And our beer was free because JB had swiped the gas card from his dad's dealership.

We often used this card for non-automotive-industry-related items. There was actually a gas station this card worked at fifteen minutes from our school that had a full meat market and liquor store inside. Therefore, many of our supplies for this trip were courtesy of the Paisley Auto Group. God bless the automotive industry.

Only myself, Jimmy, and an oddly refocused JB remained awake as we neared Big Bend National Park, in South Texas. The dog incident had given JB fresh resolve for arriving at our destination intact. We stopped to stretch our legs and get more supplies.

While JB paid, we pulled the dog's leg and an ear out of the grill of the van. Williams got obsessed with the leg. He demanded to keep it and kept tapping each of us on the shoulder with it when he needed another beer, but we had to confiscate it from him when he used it to wave to a smiling toddler who was waving at us. The kid's smile immediately turned to tears, and we pitched the dog's leg out the sunroof.

"That's bullshit, guys!" yelled Williams. "I was going to have the coolest backscratcher in town! Thanks for fucking that up."

With the canine entertainment behind us, it was time for us to do what we loved most: argue.

1997 may not have been a heavily political year as far as DC was concerned, but we always managed to argue politics as if the balance of the nation hung on the president's every move. George Herbert Walker Bush, one of my heroes, did not make the cut in 1992, as our nation decided that a hillbilly from Arkansas who played the sax on Arsenio was a more viable candidate. I like the sax, and I like some hillbillies. I just don't like Democrats.

I actually had the honor of meeting President Bush when he was VP for Reagan. He stepped out of line to take a picture with me before he began a speech, but my camera froze. He told me that if I could get my camera working before he left, he'd try his hardest to take a picture with me. When his speech ended, I thought for sure he had forgotten me, but he scanned the room, pointed me out to the Secret Service, came over, and took a picture with me. I have a lot of respect for that. The second-most-powerful man in the world didn't forget some dumb promise he made to a kid.

Last year, in 1996, the aforementioned hillbilly beat out Bob Dole, whom I had loved. Dole was mean, a bit of a hatchet man. I had hoped Dole would hatchet the Democrats, but my hopes were in vain.

I'd been raised to despise Democrats, and it had always been very easy for me. It went something like this: Republicans work hard and pay the majority of taxes. Democrats don't care *how* hard you work; they just want you to pay more taxes, because Democrats don't want to work at all. Their only wish is to take the fruits of our labor. How could any right-thinking person not hate them?

Democrats wanted to give every penny I earned to some ignorant woman on welfare who only wanted to keep having kids because every kid meant a bigger check from the government. These same folks who argued so hard for abortions somehow seemed to keep forgetting to have them.

Jimmy was our resident Democrat, and we had decided not to kill him, so, instead, we used every opportunity to debate him about how much his party sucked. Jimmy just couldn't quit stumping for Clinton, acting as though this was a guy who could balance the budget and give us eight years of prosperity.

"First of all, your boy Bush lied. Flat-out lied. He said 'no new taxes,' and what did we get? New taxes. So you wanted to vote for a liar?" Jimmy fumed.

"Maybe you should ask Hillary if Billy lied," JB snickered.

"He's a fucking snake-oil salesman," I snapped. "And Hillary is a socialist; she wants to socialize medicine. Why should I pay for other people's medical problems? Bush didn't lie; he made an error in judgment, and he had the balls to stand up and say he would have to go back on his word if he wanted to make things right."

"Can you hear yourself talking?" Jimmy asked, laughing. "Because I can. And it sounds like he lied."

"You are so misinformed," Williams said. "You're only a Democrat because you're black. You need to quit taking direction from Jesse Jackson. He's gonna drag your whole fucking race down."

"What in the fuck did you just say?" Jimmy shot back. "Do I need to get your cracker ass a white hood to wear? You need to quit taking *your* direction from Rush Limbaugh; the man is polluting your mind. And how about this Gulf War bullshit, huh? Your man Bush doesn't even know how to finish a motherfucking war. Saddam is chillin' in his house right now, drinkin' a frosty brew and screwing some hairy skank who's wearing one of those beekeeper hats or whatever. Unfinished business."

"Unfinished, my ass," I scoffed. "Saddam's been neutralized— marginalized. The man has no power. We'll never have to deal with him again. Stop being so fucking narrow-minded, and try to look at the big picture."

Just then, the van went from eighty-five to zero in as few feet as the physical universe would allow. Everyone sleeping in a seat was launched into whatever occupied the space in front of them.

"We missed our exit," JB said as he threw the van into reverse on the highway.

The debate was over.

7

We arrived at the campground just as the sun was beginning to rise. Instead of setting up tents, we decided to just sleep a couple of hours in the van and then make our trek to the rafting place, which was only about two hours away.

JB had the crazed look of someone who had just driven twelve hours while intoxicated at very high and very low rates of speed in a car splattered with dog guts. He crashed first, falling asleep without a word.

Jimmy lit a joint. "Man, you need some Jesus," he said to me.

"Do you know how fucked-up that sounds, coming from a large black man holding a joint?" I said.

"There it is again," Jim said with a sarcastic activist tone. "Black. Why can't a black man love Jesus?"

"So you're denying that you're a large black man holding a joint?" I replied in a dry tone.

"You know what I mean. Why can't a black man love Jesus?"

"I was referring to the black man with the joint."

"Screw you, man, I'm going to sleep. I know you won't need to borrow a sheet to stay warm. Just use that white one you've got on your head."

"Goodnight. I hope I've still got money in my wallet when I wake up, you fucking Democrat."

We provided the doobie with an early death and went to sleep.

To the outsider (That damn outsider again!), Jim and I might have appeared to be at each other's throats. But we weren't. That was just the nature of our friendship. We loved to argue and debate each other, and we always went for the jugular.

So many jackasses nowadays are afraid even to approach the issue of race. To do so gets them labeled as racist by people with boulder-sized chips on their shoulders. But we took it full-on. We weren't afraid to throw out insults to make our points, because we each knew we were some of the least racist dickheads around. Maybe we hadn't always been that way, but we both knew now either of us would take a bullet for the other one in an instant.

That was what made it fun for us. I could make fun of Jim for having an Afro, because he had a fucking Afro. And he could make fun of me for having a small penis, because I was white, and that was the rumor about white people or whatever.

My penis was fine, actually, but you get the picture.

We woke up after just a couple of hours' sleep, groggy but not ready yet to surrender to our bodies' yearning for rest and avoidance of further chemical imbalances.

Our plan had originally been to hike across a section of the Monahan Sand Dunes and arrive at Raging Rapids River Rafting and Outfitting on foot to begin our trek downriver via the Rio Grande. But this was looking less and less likely, as we were certain that such a hike would end shortly in a mass vomiting. So, we decided that we would just grab breakfast and drive to the damned place.

We went in search of that bastion of the redneck lifestyle, the Taj Mahal of the septic-tank-only rural elite: the Waffle House.

For those unfamiliar with a Waffle House, just think of a really old 7-Eleven and paint it yellow. Take out the aisles of candy and chips. Remove the Slurpee machine. Add tables and chairs. Then take everyone you might find wandering aimlessly around Wal-Mart at four in the morning, and stick 'em in there. Fill the air with the smoke from generic, unfiltered cigarettes. Put a really big dookie stripe in the toilet. *Boom*: the Waffle House.

It was always a good idea to try and fit in and not ruffle any feathers while in a Waffle House. We figured that the biggest way to draw attention to ourselves in such an establishment would be to dine sober, so we began passing around a bottle of Knob Creek whiskey, followed by a small joint, followed by a larger joint. By the time we arrived (our first time seeing a Waffle House in daylight), we were more than half-cocked. We fit right in.

Sometimes folks in these small Southern towns could be really shitty about having a large black guy in their midst, but in this particular joint, they seemed blasé about our mixed party. Apparently, while not in a technically advanced region of the country, these folks had somehow gotten the abolition memo.

But when Border Patrol came in and sat right next to us, eating grease carved to look like food, maybe it was just paranoia, but I thought they might take Devero away. And Devero was so fucked-up that if they hassled him, there's a decent chance that what he said might not sound like English.

The Border Patrol guys just minded their plates though, sitting there with tattered beige uniforms and an even more tattered look of *How the fuck did this happen to me?* on their faces. After a while, I was comfortable that we were in the clear and that Devero was not going to be driven "home" across the border.

Jimmy and I hadn't said much since we had woken up, and I could tell that he had some unfinished business he wanted to discuss. He had hardly finished his egg-like substance when he resumed his assault.

"So, what is it with you now, anyways?" he began. "You used to be so charismatic about going to church. You used to go every damned Wednesday and Sunday. Now you sound like a stone-cold atheist."

"I'm not an atheist," I replied. "I've told you that a thousand fucking times, dude; I'm an optimistic agnostic."

"What's the fucking difference?" he shot back.

"Well, an atheist doesn't believe in god. An agnostic believes there might be a god. An optimistic agnostic isn't sure but thinks there's a pretty good chance of it. I invented this religion, and I'm currently its only follower, but I think it might catch on."

"Optimists make me want to puke," Williams chimed in. "I don't believe in optimism or pessimism. The glass isn't half-empty or half-full. What we've got in these situations is half a glass of water. That's called being a realist."

"You sound like a fucking bumper sticker, you balding fatass," JB threw in. "Have you been reading the bumper stickers at the bong store again? Jesus, man, just get the screens and papers and leave."

Devero caught JB's eye, staring at him like the rest of us weren't there. "So I'm on a rafting trip with a fundamentalist Christian, an optimistic agnostic, and a bumper-sticker-philosophizing realist. JB, if I have to kill these sociopathic jackasses, will you help me bury the bodies?"

"No," JB answered. "I can't dig a hole big enough for Williams's fat ass, and the whole black thing would make me feel racist burying Jim. Legs, though, would be pretty easy to bury. Just stick that skinny fucker in a gopher hole. So I'm pretty much out on digging. But if I can use my joint to help you light a funeral pyre, let me know."

"Just so you know," Jimmy added, "*burning* a black man doesn't go over very well either."

"Good point," JB threw back. "But what if you're a total fucking asshole? Does that help?"

"Nope, sorry, bro. And for the record, I haven't bombed any abortion clinics lately; take it easy on the 'fundamentalist' shit. Just because a brother loves Jesus is no reason to stick him in with Jim and Tammy Faye."

It was time for a subject change. JB checked the time and told us we'd better get going if we wanted to be out on the water today.

The bill came. Williams was one of those guys that reads the bill in its entirety, taking account of every item, questioning if we'd actually gotten everything. He didn't realize that the grayish-tan matter that he had eaten was "hash browns" and had to be shown another patron's plate in order to suspend his disbelief.

Our waitress, Connie, stood her ground. She looked like she'd been through a motherfucker of a life. Her skin looked like two-inch-thick brown leather, scored with long, deep creases. She had a bad dye job on her matted hair and thick blue-and-black shit around her eyes, probably masking domestic abuse. Her fingernails were mismatched colors, and they were broken, most likely from bar fights. She looked right at home.

Williams tried to argue for a bit, but when the Border Patrol guys next to us started looking over their shoulder, Williams coughed up the dough, and we headed to the van.

"Jesus, Williams, you're such a Jew," Jimmy said in an annoyed, high-pitched tone. "Have you ever just paid a check, or do you always make an ass of yourself?"

"Jew?! Are you fucking kidding me? I'm being called a Jew by a moon cricket?"

"What in the fuck did you just say?"

This was a very common response from Jimmy, like his tagline. It was generally his reply when anything derogatory was said concerning his race. Usually, it was asked in a pissed-off but nonpoisonous tone—because he had no problem calling us *honkey*, *cracker*, *whitebread*, or pretty much any other Caucasian insult.

But Jimmy and Williams's relationship had not been built on

terra firma, and we sometimes wondered if they would actually throw down. Seeing as how Williams, one of our closest friends, was an asshole, this was one of those times.

"I said don't throw stones if you live in a black house," Williams responded.

It was as if he had gotten a full hundred-yard running start and just gracelessly leapt over that line you don't cross.

"Listen, guys," I chimed in. "We're at the very beginning of our last trip together for a while. Couldn't you guys just—"

Wham! Jimmy knocked the shit out of him.

I sure as shit didn't see it coming. Neither did Williams.

Jimmy, the teddy bear—the big, drunk, high, mushroom-eating, fundamentalist teddy bear—knocked Williams flat on his ass. I bet both his feet came off the ground.

"I accept your apology," Jimmy mumbled as he walked away.

"Suck it," Williams replied. Apparently, Jimmy hadn't knocked the asshole out of him.

"Well, that's settled," JB said.

And so we left.

So I guess this is one of those tension-building points in the story. You can see that finely illustrated by (A) Jimmy and me having monumental clashes on both partisan and religious issues and (B) Jimmy knocking the ever-loving shitballs out of Williams for being even more of an overwhelming asshole than usual and crossing lines that build unwanted racial turmoil. Generally, this is done after you've gotten to know some of the inner workings of all characters involved in a story. That's so you can decide whose side you want to take.

I'm not sure that's the way this story works.

Sometimes, it takes a trip like this for someone's character to truly be revealed, so you can't really know it yet. *I* couldn't really know it yet. I like all of my friends. I don't want you to feel antipathy toward any of them—even Williams. Because, while Williams was obviously quite obtuse and had a terrible attitude toward life, he was our friend. He would jump in front of a train for us. Well, maybe not. That's probably a stretch. But he would probably tell us if a train was coming as he was walking to safety.

Williams had always been the most difficult member of the group. He was the kind of guy who would say absolutely anything to absolutely anyone. He would hit on pregnant chicks. He would walk around parties with his balls hanging out of his zipper. He would pee in the "trash-can punch." When he ran out of beer, he would drink that very same punch he'd just pissed in. He once asked a poorly dressed substitute teacher whether he had gotten his socks for free with a bowl of soup at the night shelter. He was just that kind of guy. He was born on third base and told everyone he'd hit a triple. What did he have to worry about? He had his parents' credit card to travel around the country for a while when we got back. And when he felt like starting work, he had a job lined up that would start him off at a hundred grand a year. His dad would buy him a new house and a new car, and he would most likely breeze through the rest of his asshole life without a worry.

So, why was he so cheap? Well, he just always thought everyone was out to get him. He thought everyone wanted to screw him out of his money. He was almost paranoid. No, wait. He *was* paranoid. And he was embarrassing. And he was vile. And he was unlovable. But aren't we all sometimes?

Whenever I thought about why we kept Williams around, I always thought about the dummies. Quite possibly, our finest acts as miscreants in college were the dummies.

The dummies provided us with a rare glimpse into the psyche of someone involved in extreme circumstances. For instance, have you ever seen the look on the face of someone who thinks they've just witnessed a person being run over by a truck? I have. Actually, I have it on video. It's priceless. Horrible when you lend much thought to it, but priceless.

We had become professionals at taking old clothing and man-
nequin heads from a beauty salon owned by Williams's aunt and
making them look like a real person.

More to the point, a real *dead* person.

We would leave them in the street with guts made of spaghetti
and tomato sauce thrown on top and then we would hide in the
bushes, sometimes even on campus. The incidents made both local
and campus newspapers. It was very morbid but good for a laugh
for the spiritually downtrodden.

On our last and most fulfilling "dummy day," the sky was blue,
the sun was shining, and life was great—or as great as it could be
for an unhappy, self-conscious, spiritually void being such as I was.

We were upset that Williams couldn't join our adventure that
day. Generally, we all did everything in our power to be there. But
he said he had something to do. Little did we know, we'd be seeing
Williams soon enough.

Everything was a go.

Dummy in position? Check.

Guts looking nasty? Check.

Good hiding spot? Check.

Video rolling? Check.

Then the fun began. The cars began to stop. All in all, there must
have been seven or eight cars stopped at a distance from the dummy,
with a few folks on car phones calling the proper authorities. No
one was getting close. And *dammit*, it looked just like a dead person
in the road.

We were so busy watching their faces and laughing that we never
even saw Williams coming.

There was this heavyset lady in an old Cadillac who was really
not dealing well with the situation. As she inched a bit closer
to inspect the damage, she heard the glasspacks on Williams's
truck's exhaust screaming, and she looked up to see his big blue

Chevy truck on the horizon, barreling down the street. He hit the dummy doing about sixty. The look on the faces in the crowd really said it all.

We were speechless. We were all just so proud of him. In a single swooping motion, he had increased the emotional impact of our little project exponentially. It was the best dummy job we'd ever done. We never even tried to top it.

10

I've always felt like maybe we weren't going to make it—you know, as a civilization. Maybe it's not the healthiest outlook to have. But really, how are we going to do it?

And it's that fear . . . We've all seen the video of the mushroom cloud. It's terrible. It's terrible to think about—for you to know I think about it. I never want anything to happen to any of my family or friends. I worry about them all so much; I want to be the first to go. But I worry I'll be the last.

So I guess I've always hated tension. I've always been the mediator. At a young age, and even more recently, after my parents would have a particularly loud argument, I would counsel them about the ways in which divorce tears families apart.

I know that, at any moment, tragedy could strike.

Jimmy's father and brother were evidence of that. One minute, you're enjoying yourself; the next, you've been erased. That, my friend, is the terminal rigidity of life.

But I always fought to keep people together, bound by something not so tangible as we might like sometimes. Everybody is fucked-up somehow, but we've got to find what can bind us. It's too easy to find reasons not to like people.

I knew my role as resident therapist might now be beckoned to ease the situation between Williams and Jimmy. Additionally, I do believe that when Jimmy knocked the shit out of Williams, his politicoreligious skirmish with me was cast aside—trumped.

I knew I had my work cut out for me here. I mean, Williams called Jimmy a moon cricket, and Jimmy lifted Williams off of the ground with a lightning-quick uppercut. Racism and violence. Dammit, why does it always come down to that?

"Excuse me, guys," I began as we pulled away in the van. "We need to address the whole Jew/moon cricket/uppercut thing. Haven't we been through enough shit together by now? I'd like to leave the tension convention now. Could you guys please kiss and make up?"

"I'll take a blow job," JB called from the driver's seat.

"From who?" asked Williams.

"Not to show any preferential treatment," JB replied, "but I'd prefer Jimmy. His goatee will make it easier to use my imagination. Plus, I've never been with a black man before."

"Oh yeah, that's how it all starts," Jimmy shot back. "First we act like friends. Then we throw out a little 'moon cricket' here and there. Next thing you know, you're asking a brother to blow you. If only the good Reverend Jackson could see you people now."

"First of all," I said, "there are no television cameras around, so Jesse ain't coming. Second, what's with this 'you people' shit? Have you no recollection of Ross Perot? Seriously, man. Not cool."

"Always gotta go after Jesse," Jimmy said, shaking his head. "You know those hostages he got released were white, don't you? Still not good enough, though, huh? 'He's got a 'fro, he's got to go,' right? And why the hell are you bitching about Ross Perot? Do y'all motherfuckers really need super-short members in the Klan? Him being gone from the political climate is goddamn Darwinian."

"Sweet Jesus, Jim, the hypocrisy is just blinding," I sighed. "I'm just trying to bring people together here, man, and you want to get back into the political arena. Fine. How come it's okay for Jesse Jackson to use the term *Hymietown*, but you knocked Williams's nose sideways for calling you a moon cricket, *after* you called him a Jew? On what planet does that make sense?"

"Okay, no need to bring the Savior into this," Jimmy said, holding up his hands, palms out. "But Williams isn't Jewish, at least not on paper. That shit is different."

"So I can call Williams a moon cricket?"

"Yes. But I'm still not giving JB a BJ."

"I'm lost," said Devero.

"You're not alone," I told him. "Jimmy is practicing a typical Democrat tactic right now, called *deflection*. It's meant to confuse. You see, Democrats work from a very complex playbook, in which the rules don't necessarily apply to them.

"For example," I continued, "look at the role race plays in the two parties currently destroying our country. The Democrats call the Republicans racist, just like Jimmy is doing now. They grab every soapbox and hog every microphone to let you know that the Republicans are white supremacists. Yet which party has really ever done anything about civil rights? Which party has put women and black people in positions of power? Who put a black man on the Supreme Court? The rules don't apply to the Democrats. They just want handouts; they just want to perpetuate the situation that many black people now find themselves in.

"They don't want to give a man a fish, and they don't want to teach him to fish," I said heatedly. "They just think some people are 'owed' fucking fish, and it pisses me off."

"Wow. You really do buy into your party's bullshit, don't you?"

Jimmy said. "So let's examine why black folks have the problems they have. First of all, they were taken away from their rightful homes in another part of the world and sold like animals for hard labor.

"White people killed off anyone who wanted to learn or succeed or be free. They kept the ones who kept their heads down, shut up, and worked. Black slaves *built* this country yet were never allowed to reap any of the benefits. They built many of these corporations and share none of the wealth. They were beaten, hanged, raped, humiliated. And then one day, the white people said, 'Okay, we're not allowed to own you anymore, so go be free—but not in *my* neighborhood. And I don't care what your people went through; we're not going to help you be equal. Freedom to live in poverty should be enough for you. At least you're not living in the jungle anymore.'

"So you wanna know why we grab a microphone when we can? Because *we helped build this country*. We bled for it as slaves. And for too long, we were quiet. But now we want a piece of it." Jimmy turned around in his seat, locking eyes with me in our typical "your turn, bitch" way.

"Give me a break," I said. "You're talking about reparations now. That's where you're steering this. You think that a bunch of white people who never owned slaves should give a huge chunk of money to a bunch of black people who've never been slaves? How does that possibly make sense?"

"We did it for the Jews and the Japanese," Jimmy pointed out.

"Yeah, but they were still alive."

"So it's okay for the white ancestors of corporations to continue to acquire wealth from work that both white and black people did long ago, but it's not okay for black ancestors of slaves owned by those corporations to acquire some of that same wealth?"

"Well, then, I guess the black race would sign over their checks to the Jews, right?" I retorted. "Because the Jews were slaves to the Africans. And as slaves to the Africans, they did a few small things like, oh, you know, building the pyramids. So are you willing to sign over your check?"

"Kiss my black ass, man. I'm tired of this shit," Jimmy said, leaning forward in his seat. "Hey, JB, how long till this traveling Klan rally makes it to the river?"

JB glared back at us, obviously annoyed.

"Well, for a few minutes, I thought for sure that I would be killing myself long before we got there. We're close now—a couple of miles from the exit. If you guys are done arguing, I think I'll wait and kill myself by the river; it will be both beautiful and poetic."

11

'd had another college lined up originally. In fact, I had even got a partial scholarship for art, which was where my heart was. I was going to be a double major in art and philosophy, although my father said that the job market in both fields was slim. Of course, he was right. But originally, he was going to pay for what the scholarship didn't cover. Then he changed his mind, probably because I got arrested.

In the middle of the summer after high school, Devero, Jimmy, Williams, and I had been out late drinking and doing "yard jobs"—which consisted of driving into people's front lawns and doing "donuts," tearing up their yards in a major way and making miniature crop circles.

We ran out of cigarettes at some point during the off-road performance-driving exercise, and that's when things got ugly. We pulled up to our local Food Sack grocery store, next to the pretending-to-be-upscale Dove's Furniture, in wonderful Hurst, Texas. Jimmy and Williams hopped out of the car, presumably to go buy some smokes. Devero and I stayed in the vehicle, and I lit a roach from the ashtray.

We were laughing about events that had occurred earlier in the day, with these local girls we had booty-called. All of our laughter must have masked the commotion going on outside the vehicle.

We didn't even think twice when Williams leaned in the window and said, "Open the trunk."

Not too long after that, Jimmy and Williams climbed back into our mud-covered chariot. We didn't even get out of the parking lot before a fleet of police cruisers surrounded us. Only then did I look across at Dove's Furniture.

Jimmy and Williams had pretty much destroyed the front of the building—not to mention put some keepsakes in the trunk, making this what they call in the realm of law enforcement "an open-and-shut case."

"Eat the weed, guys," Devero calmly ordered.

"What about the mushrooms?" asked Williams.

"Fuck . . . We'll have to eat those, too," Devero muttered.

In a matter of seconds, we had eaten too much weed and too many mushrooms.

Devero then delivered a second blow of bad news. "I've got a warrant out for my arrest," he said. "For speeding. I never paid the tickets. I'm going to have to pretend I'm my brother and say I forgot my license. Legs, hold my driver's license."

And so I did.

Let me add at this point that the Hurst Police had a reputation for being very tough rednecks. They weren't fans of anyone who didn't wear a cowboy hat or know how to gut a deer with a pocket-knife in under four minutes.

The first police officer to approach us went over to Devero, who was in the driver's seat.

"Licencia y el seguro, por favor," the officer said to him.

"Dude, I'm fucking American, okay? I'm just tan," Devero responded.

"Oh. Sorry. License and insurance, please."

"I'm afraid I don't have my license on me."

"What's your name?"

"Chris Devero."

Shit. He was supposed to say "Ken," his brother's name, but I guess either the Spanish threw him off, or the mushrooms kicked in entirely too early. You'd think he'd be used to the Spanish by now.

And so they ran his real name. The news wasn't good.

"I'm afraid you're going to have to come with me," said the cop. "Step out of the vehicle."

"Don't worry," I told Devero. "I'll take your car back, and we'll get some money together for—"

And then my door opened. That wasn't supposed to happen.

"Everyone out of the vehicle," said the cop. "Everyone up against the wall."

Now came a time that I secretly enjoyed. In moments of crisis, and other times when the situation called for it, my friends had always looked to me to be the "talker." It seems as though my language skills are able to adapt to any vernacular, that I can speak as one of the people, with excellent enunciation and extraordinary manners. This is something I inherited from my father, although he used his powers for good.

"I believe there's been a misunderstanding here, sir," I said, with just the proper amount of Southern drawl. "Why are we being talked to as if we've committed a crime?" I hoped to appeal to their redneck sensibilities, and in my mind, I began to prepare an excellent large-mouth bass story.

"Shut the fuck up," snapped the cop. "You guys been drinking? Do I smell marijuana?"

"A couple of us had a beer at a party earlier, but no drugs. No, sir. We're not a bunch of dopers. I've seen that stuff destroy too many lives."

"Uh-huh," the cop grunted. It was more of a *Yeah, right, jackass* than actual agreement.

"What is it that you think we've done, sir?" I tried again. "I'd like to get this straightened out."

"Once again, shut the fuck up," the cop growled. "You guys are so smart that you parked approximately thirty feet away from a security truck with a guard inside. He saw the whole thing. It's gonna be tough for me to believe you when you have contraband from this vandalized store in your trunk."

I must say, the guy made sense. My talking abilities were blocked from reaching their potential. It sucked being shut down by a redneck.

And so, it was off to jail. Everyone's mushroom trip came on pretty strong at about the time we were being "cuffed and stuffed." It made our ride to the station all the more interesting. One thing I can definitely recommend if you're ever in police custody in the rear of a cop car is not to repeatedly ask if the computer screen in the cruiser has Nintendo. The more you ask, the angrier they will get. And never—and I mean *never*—piss on the floor of the cop car. That *really* rubs them the wrong way.

Unfortunately, we did both. You can't really blame us, though, because we were hard in the grips of the fungus. The fungus was among us.

We got thrown into two separate holding cells. I was thrown in with Jimmy. Devero was thrown in with Williams. I tried to reason with Jimmy, since Devero and I were essentially innocent and since Devero had the most to lose, on account of his warrant.

"Listen, Jimmy. Devero and I never even got out of the car. You've gotta tell the cops that we weren't involved."

Jimmy looked at me strangely, sort of the way a fish in an aquarium looks at a person outside the glass. I could tell that I wasn't getting through, but I continued.

"C'mon, man. Just tell the cops, and—"

I was interrupted by a new friend, a cop who stood no shorter than six foot six and weighed no less than 350 pounds. He had the requisite cop mustache and a balding flattop haircut—the kind where there's just a tuft of hair in the front, but it's flat enough to set your clock to—and an angry red face.

"Hey, kid," boomed the cop, "why don't you just sit down and shut the fuck up? Take your medicine. You did the crime, now you'll do the time."

Nobody really knows what came over me at that instant. It was one of those chemically induced moments of courage where you rise to the occasion, even though the occasion may not quite call for it.

"Were you there?" I asked, standing up and approaching the behemoth.

"What?" he responded, shocked as hell.

"Were you there, on the scene, when the crime occurred?" I got right up in his face.

"No."

"Were you even there afterward, during the arrests?" This time, I poked him in the chest as I asked.

"No."

"Were you at all involved in any of this?" I poked again.

"No."

"Well then, why don't *you* sit down and shut the fuck up? You aren't qualified to be in this conversation."

As I went for my final poke, for a bit of point emphasis, the cop grabbed my arm and threw me against the wall. He twisted me into somewhere between a half and full nelson, perhaps a three-quarter nelson. Then his big red face got right in mine.

"You'd better pray to God and sonny Jesus that I never meet you in a dark alley," he snarled quietly in my ear.

"I don't hang out in dark alleys," I retorted. "Do you hang out in dark alleys? That's fucked-up—you being a cop, hanging out in dark alleys for pervy fetish shit . . ."

I thought at that moment I had perhaps taken my last breath, but the guy was so incredibly mad that he had to slowly let go and back out of the room. I had broken something in his head. He was just as confused as he was pissed off. But he left.

Williams didn't help the matter by letting his pants fall around his ankles while being photographed for his mug shot by a female officer. They'd taken his belt so he wouldn't hang himself in his cell. He wasn't wearing underwear.

We all had to take a moment to regain what little composure we were capable of as the flashbulbs went off. Flashbulbs either *do* or *do not* go well with psychedelic mushrooms. It's all a matter of context; you know, it's situational. But there's not a lot of middle ground. I think Devero actually tried to *catch* the light from the flash.

After we were processed, Williams, Jimmy, and I were placed in one cell, with Devero in an adjoining cell next to ours. Our cellmate was sort of a cross between the lead singer of Metallica and Charles Manson. He appeared comatose, sleeping on the quasi bunk bed that stuck out like a shelf from the wall. There was a single metal toilet in the middle of the room, which put my normal toilet-masturbation routine on hiatus.

At one point, I hocked a big loogie from across the cell toward the toilet in an attempt to score a toilet goal. The rather embryonic-looking large loogie came to rest on the seat of the toilet. Not too long after that, our resident serial killer/heavy metal singer awoke from his slumber, traversed the cell to the toilet, sat down, and took a dump. He didn't bother to wipe the seat. He just sat on my little embryo.

Devero's cellmates were a pack of wild Hispanics. They probably placed him with them so he could get an early start with a good Latin gang. The only English that the Latino guys appeared to know was "The toilet no work."

It actually did work, we found out later, after they were released. They probably just didn't want to smell any fecal matter over and above what they had already produced. Or they just didn't want to watch Devero shit. Hell, none of us did.

We apparently began making quite a bit of noise in our cells as the night rolled on. We hit the "call" button with fierce repetitiveness. Just because we were locked in a room didn't mean we couldn't party. I believe that the police in that station began to wish that they hadn't brought us in. But since they had, they now had to break up the party. They separated us into four different cells, at the four farthest corners of the jail.

My new cellmate was Marvin. Marvin was a nice, intelligent man whose interests included assault and armed robbery. He was awaiting transfer to a maximum-security prison.

We met with the judge the following morning. We were being held on two felonies—criminal theft and criminal vandalism—and one misdemeanor, minor in possession of alcohol. I was being charged with an extra misdemeanor for carrying a fake ID—the one Devero asked me to hold on to as this long, strange trip took flight. Our bail had been set at five thousand dollars apiece, because, as the judge told us, we had showed an amazing level of disrespect for authority. I finally called my dad after exhausting every other adult I had ever encountered who might have access to five thousand dollars cash. He provided me with an incredible display of telepathy. He knew by the tone of my voice before I said it that I was in the hoosegow.

He had a friend at the bank meet him to get the cash. He came and got me, with my mom in tow. As we exited the correctional facility, I began to speak but was interrupted by an alarmingly quick blow to the face.

My old man had just clocked me.

It wasn't the first time, and it wouldn't be the last. I certainly deserved it.

It was that day that my father told me that he would not pay for any more of my craziness. He would not pay for me to abuse him further at the college I wanted to go to. He would not pay for college at all. I was now on my own. I was off the tit.

I told them I guess I would have to join the Air Force. I thought for sure this would scare them into paying for college again, but my dad didn't say anything. This was, after all, when the Gulf War had just been big news. I mentioned the tension in the Middle East. They remained silent.

I even went so far as to invite the recruiter over to the house a few days later to discuss things. We talked about the many ways in which the USAF could help me achieve my goals. I led the conversation toward combat, because I knew my mother was listening from the other room. I thought surely this would do the trick. But no. She didn't break.

It was time to play my ace. I called my mother one morning and let her know that today was the day. I was signing up at noon. If my parents didn't stop me, I was absolutely going to join the armed forces. But the call didn't come.

I entered the recruiter's office at noon exactly. I sat in the waiting room.

Just as the recruiter opened the door to let me in, my dad's super-sized cell phone that he let me borrow rang. It was my dad. I told the recruiter that I needed to take this call, that it was urgent. I could tell he wanted me in basic training, under his direct supervision. He nodded, and I stepped outside.

"Where are you?" asked my dad.

"At the recruiter's office, signing up," I replied.

He let out the sigh of a beaten man. "Okay, you win. You've played a nice hand. I'll pay for you to go to Texas Methodist."

I walked directly to my car. I didn't even tell the recruiter goodbye. I wondered how many times that guy had seen someone excuse themselves for a phone call, never to see that person again. I strongly felt there was something waiting for me somewhere else. Maybe it was my talk show. But I just didn't see the military in my grand plan.

Going to the local school, Texas Methodist University, didn't bother me much. I didn't have to pay for it. I didn't have to go through basic training. My father liked it because I could focus on taking over his business, as the school had an excellent business program for real estate. He should have been more worried that it was where all my friends were going.

FRIENDSHIP HATE MODER
OCRISY HEROISM DRUGS IMMO
RICANS SANCTITY LOYALTY CON
INTOLERANCE HIGH TURMOIL DI
RITUALITY DISAFFECTED TURBU
MPTION DEATH ACCEPTANCE LUD
ATEFUL FALLING ROCK 'N ROLL T
GHTING QUESTIONS ALCOHOL POI
ONVERGING PHILOSOPHY MUSHRO
NREASONABLE LIFE YOUTH ISOLA
OURAGE WEED DEFIANCE EVOLUTI
RSEVERANCE DEPRESSION DELUS
NATURAL SELECTION LAUGHTER
PAIR ORDEAL DETERMINATION D
ADVENTURE IGNORANCE MIND A
RIENCE JUDGEMENT UNEASE N
ATED MAGNIFICENT ANTICI

PART II
The Bending of Light

"We have arrived," JB said. "Grab your shit, and let's roll."

Reeking of alcohol and weed, it was up to me, the "designated talker," to convince these border dwellers that we were responsible enough to navigate their expensive boating equipment downstream.

I squirted a half bottle of Visine in each eye, put on my sunglasses, and popped a couple of tearjerkingly strong mints into my mouth.

I approached the modified shed that was home to RRRRO, LLC, otherwise known as Raging Rapids River Rafting and Outfitting. I wondered what the hell they outfitted, because it sure as hell wasn't this shithole. I guess there's a lot to be said for low overhead, though. Had there been a door, I would've opened it as I walked in.

Legs Hamilton, on in three . . . two . . . one . . .

"Hola, muchacho. Wassappennin?" said the nice man behind the counter.

"Hola. We're a few minutes late, but we have a reservation for a five-day/four-night ride down the Rio Grande. The name is Hamilton. We're going down to your farthest checkpoint, and then you guys are supposed to drive us back here, right?"

"How may I helping you?" he asked.

God bless him. Perhaps if my talk show ever goes bilingual or we want to do some Hispanic cross marketing, I can come back for this guy. But it was time to simplify things.

"Here's our cash," I said. "Dónde the uh . . . boats?"

Cash and *boats*—he had heard those before. What a waste of Visine. There were obviously no requirements except cash needed here. I filled out the paperwork, forging everyone's initials on the damage and injury waivers, and we were in business.

13

I had a lot of time to think on the way down there. Sure, my judgment may have been a bit impaired, but such is life.

I was having a hard time enjoying myself. I just couldn't help thinking about going to work. I was actually going to be a "Joe Punchclock." I would be Brian Hamilton, no longer Legs, and I would have a business card that reflected that. How did this happen?

It happened because I let it. I could have been my own man if I'd gone into the military. Or if I had actually gotten a job (*What?*) and tried to pay for what my art scholarship didn't cover. But I had to take the easy way, and this is what the easy way gave me. It gave me something, but not enough. It didn't give me what I wanted. I had always been so angry, almost as if I were owed what I wanted without any sacrifice on my part. But that's not where all of the anger came from. A lot of it came from that same age-old shit: I was the little guy getting knocked around. It's such a horrible, bullshit thing to go through. Always, everywhere, when you spoke up, you got your legs swept out from under you.

For the most part, with few exceptions, teachers had always been especially hard on me. I don't know if I've illustrated that sufficiently. Much of what they did was self-righteous indignation and bullying—as if the student bullies didn't bully me enough. They refused to listen to me. And this did not come from traditional methods of *tough love*; it came from traditional methods of *asshole*.

I know that at least some of it came from my parents being moderately wealthy; everyone hates a rich kid. But a lot of it came from my raising challenging issues for them and them being unwilling or unable to meet the challenges. I became an outspoken voice in the high school newspaper editorials, fighting for the right to wear our hair the way we wanted, fighting for looser uniform restrictions, etc. I was also the newspaper cartoonist and would raise my issues there as well.

Our school carried on the tradition of Hell Week—or "Welcome Week," as they liked to call it. It was generally good-natured, duct-taping-freshmen-to-the-bathroom-wall type of fun, the kind of fun all of us skinny kids might cry quietly about as we cleaned our guns and looked for razor blades. As in life outside of parochial school, sometimes someone just takes shit too far. Usually, that someone was me. But not this time.

Bob Lapoza was quite possibly the largest senior at our school. And like many knuckle-dragging linebackers of his ilk, he thought that the best way to display his muscles was to pick on the smallest guy in school. I had the honor of being that guy. I still remember locking eyes with this gent as I entered the lunchroom one day during Hell Week. He spoke with such dignity; it was almost as if he had been temporarily possessed by the ghost of Ernest Hemingway.

"Hey, you pussy little freshman fag. Get over here," he said.

"Who, me?" I asked, trembling in fear.

"Any other little pussy gaywad freshmen in here?" he demanded.

"I don't know. Give me a minute, and I'll check," I answered, hoping the Jedi mind trick would work. It didn't.

"I'm thirsty. I need you to pour my drink in my mouth for me so the newspaper girl can take a picture of it."

"You've got to be fucking kidding me. Didn't you learn how to do this already? Didn't somebody, at some point in time, cover this material?"

"Get over here now, homo, before I kick your little pansy ass."

Wow. He sure had a way with words.

I don't know if the presence of the newspaper photographer had anything to do with my next actions, but maybe. It was such a mixed blessing, in hindsight. But this was my life, what I had become accustomed to. I was the little guy who got beat up. That was my role.

So it probably shocked the shit out of Bob Lapoza when I took his drink and threw it in his face. It probably shocked him even more when the newspaper ran the picture of this in action on the front page. He was quite possibly most shocked when I drew the experience into a cartoon for the newspaper. Lastly, it probably shocked no one when Bob Lapoza beat the shit out of me.

Every one of my friends on the rafting trip had jumped in to help me. And, consequently, they had all got their asses beat as well.

I just wished I could have shown a clip of that drink-throwing incident on the talk show. I would edit out the ass beating, of course.

But I loved the newspaper. The newspaper offered me a voice. I loved the way all the students eagerly awaited my next cartoon or editorial. Mrs. Anglin, the head of the Journalism Department, hated my group of friends, as did most faculty and staff. But she saved that special, white-hot hate for me.

I had been drawing newspaper cartoons for three and a half years when she fired me. Our other cartoonist had been stealing cartoons from Gary Larson's *The Far Side* and calling them his own, and due to liability issues brought on by this dipshit, she fired the entire cartooning staff—both of us. She said plagiarism was too big a liability, as if Gary Larson himself were poised to take the school for all it had.

This was an easy way for her to take away the students' voice, the voice that was tarnishing her star pupil's image. Really, she did it just to piss me off.

Going to work for my dad in real estate seemed like having my voice taken away all over again. I was now going to go against what everyone always says: "Follow your dreams. Find a job you love."

How many people really do that, anyway?

I think the people they bring to schools to preach such tripe should be tied to horses and dragged through town, for all of the folks who didn't follow their dreams to gloat over.

And when they are cut free, they should be beaten.

14

Getting loaded up on the boats was actually relatively easy. We were so late that the normal crew had gone home already, which meant only the clerk (whose name we discovered was Jorge) was still around to send us off. From a liability standpoint, this was perhaps not a bright move, but it allowed us to load up more quickly—and most likely less safely—and within minutes we were ready to push off.

We hadn't discussed yet who would man the Q boat—so named because it carried all of our camping and eating equipment. I always thought "E boat" seemed more applicable, but I also thought the guy handing you helmets and advice should be an effective communicator, so what the hell do I know?

If you've ever been on a long rafting trip, you are familiar with the Q boat. If not, keep reading. Actually, keep reading anyhow.

The Q boat was the same size as the boat meant for people—about twelve feet long. The difference is that, instead of a passenger area, the Q had just one seat, perched in the middle, with long paddles secured in holsters; the rest of the boat was for equipment storage. The operator of the Q boat had a different task from the occupants of the passenger boat. He had to handle the whole boat alone, through calm water and through rapids, risking being the asshole who lost everything. The other boat would be the fun one. There was one man up front, one on each side, and one in the back. First, we decided that the Q boat would be an alternating position. Then we began to lay out the reasons why each of us shouldn't be the first one to take a turn.

"I've been driving all night. Fuck you guys, I'm last," JB said.

We had to admit, the guy had a point. He was immediately cleared of duty.

"I'll get shot by Border Patrol if I'm seen alone," Devero suggested.

A shaky argument at best. He would have to man the Q boat at some point, and we would be on the border the whole way.

"Jimmy and I just came off a hard bender," I announced. "We've been drinking for days. I think it would be a bad idea for either of us."

"Also, my hand hurts," said Jimmy.

"My face hurts," added Williams.

It was a four-way tie.

"Time for a dick-measuring contest," said JB.

"That's not fair! Jimmy's got the advantage," Devero said.

"Well, I win that one," Jimmy added, recusing and excusing himself.

That made it a three-way tie. The best way to handle a three-way tie is known to everyone. You know it before you read it. Rock, paper, scissors, odd man out.

And I was the odd man out.

Shit.

15

I looked over at the other boat. The guys were all gathering floating moss and making big, wet, nasty balls out of it. This could
only mean trouble. Not only was I a sitting duck on my raised seat,
but I was also too high up to make any of my own mossballs, since
the engineers of the Q boat had the opinion that you should be able
to see more shit when you were the Lone Ranger.

I held up Devero and Williams's backpacks, one in each arm,
sending the message that I was willing to use their shit as a shield
should they choose a preemptive strike.

"Okay, okay, chill," called Williams. "No need to get ugly. Put
down the packs."

"Black man, Fatass, Monkey Arms, Jihadi . . . Drop your mossballs in the water," I ordered.

They all seemed to understand my language of mutually assured
destruction. They dropped their weapons, and I lowered the packs.

Whack! Right in the head. Fucking Williams.

This was going to suck.

I climbed down to the edge of the boat to rinse the moss out of my ear and off of my face. I noticed that the water was already picking up speed a bit. Soon, we would be going over some decent rapids, the only rough water we would hit that day.

I'd been on a number of rafting trips with these guys: Steamboat Springs, Jackson Hole, Durango, Indian Creek. But none of us had ever manned our own Q boat before. We had always had guides. We had to get a game plan together if we expected to survive.

"Hey, guys," I called out, "we've got some class 3s coming up. Jorge said something about rain earlier, and something about class 4s. Do you guys remember what he said exactly? Anyone?"

"Nada."

"Didn't catch it."

"No comprende."

"Well, I think the formation should be the Q boat first, with you guys lined up following just in case I lose control," I stated with mild confidence. "Just like we all lined up behind Williams's mom after he passed out at graduation. Don't get too close and bump me, or you'll turn me. And somebody throw me a beer."

Williams, ever the asshole, whipped a Keystone Light tallboy at me with blistering speed and startling precision. I caught the beer as if I'd been training for months. It was kind of a fuck-you catch. It felt great. People like me, with no athletic skills, relish moments like that. I was waiting for a "Nice catch!" but they were collectively unimpressed. I cracked the beer open and sized things up.

What the fuck had Jorge even said? Damn you, Jorge. It was a combination of us not paying attention and Jorge's lack of fluency in the language that had made the conversation such a failure. From the looks of things, I was beginning to be sure that he said that the first set of rapids was running especially fierce. As we floated along, the water was getting rougher and rougher.

"Everybody get your life jackets on! It's about to get nuts!" I yelled.

I slammed my beer and threw the can into the boat. I grabbed my bag of Red Man Golden Blend and quickly crammed an oversized plug in my cheek. This was definitely a Red Man time.

If you've never chewed tobacco, you should. I also recommend that you get your children, if you have them, to start chewing at a very early age. Not only is it amazingly good for making your lips and cheeks more pliable, but it forces onlookers to respect you.

After stuffing Instant Manliness into my cheek, I buckled my life jacket on and said a quick optimistic-agnostic prayer.

"Hey, jackasses!" I screamed. "Stay farther back! If you rub my boat, you'll turn me!"

Oh, that was the more fun boat for sure. The rapids were roaring and the scenery was flying by, with dips and dunks and eddies and whirls everywhere. But the other guys' level of seriousness did not reflect their surroundings. They were laughing their asses off with their life jackets unbuckled. Carefree.

I, on the other hand, was using every muscle in my one-hundred-thirty-seven-pound frame to keep this boat straight so that I didn't flip, which would send our equipment downstream and most assuredly kill me.

Not far from the edge of the first rather massive waterfall, the guys forgot my request and bumped the Q boat in an unfortunate spot.

"Sorry about that, bro. My bad. Was that like my mom also?" Williams shouted in his cockiest voice.

"No, dickhead, your mom's a hell of a lot bigger than that boat. And I promise I bumped into her a lot more than once," I yelled back.

The river narrowed a bit here, and my only option was to hit the one nice opening perfectly straight. But since the guys had bumped me, I was instead heading for the large boulder on the left, sideways. Damned if I didn't try for the opening anyway though. I was delusional for a very brief, almost immeasurable moment. I thought I might just make it. Instead, I hit the boulder decently hard—well, hard enough to throw me out of my seat and over the side of the boat.

Thankfully, I was able to grab the rope that encircled the boat. But the side of the boat was still up against the boulder, and it was rising higher and higher out of the water.

The boat was about to flip over on me.

Since I figured that our shit was going to get wet anyhow, I decided there was no reason to have it land on my head first. So I let go.

I was making the conscious decision to go over class 4 rapids with all of the safety and security of a life jacket.

Just after I had made the decision to kill myself in this brutal fashion, the other guys decided it was time for them to go over the falls as well. They had managed to hang on to the boulder on the right. I don't know how they mustered the strength to stay there for that long, seeing as how they were all in tears from laughing at me.

I mean, they were really laughing. Uncontrollably.

I went over the falls perhaps ten or fifteen feet in front of them. I tried to keep my feet in front of me, as they always tell you to do. But I had to keep looking back at the guys in the other boat.

I was dumbfounded. I had hoped to see some concern in their eyes, but mostly all I saw was wild laughter.

I went over waterfall after waterfall, banging around from boulder to boulder, nearly drowning every few feet, crying out to the nearest available god to prove himself to me, screaming in terror. The guys followed close behind, no more than fifteen feet the whole time.

All I saw from them was gut-wrenching, tearjerking, knee-slapping laughter. It was a disgusting display. Not once did it appear to cross their minds that they should try to save me. I was far too valuable as entertainment.

The good news was that the Q boat had not flipped after all. We saw it popping wildly down the falls behind us. I should have hung on. That was probably something Jorge covered.

To make matters worse, this turned out not to be a good time for Red Man after all. As I was swallowing water by the gallon, I also swallowed my large glob of tobacco. I started throwing up as I went over the last few falls, trying to keep my feet in front of me and not get puke on my face.

I could hear really high-pitched laughter now, painful laughter. They had reached the ceiling on how hard they could laugh.

God, strike them down. Please.

16

After the water calmed down a bit, I took inventory of myself. I was floating closer to the boat now. I felt around for gaping wounds. I didn't appear to have any broken bones, just a few scrapes and bruises.

The other guys refused to pull me up onto their boat, saying it was my responsibility to regain the helm of the Q boat. I knew they didn't want me on their boat because of the vomit, so I assured them that I had washed it all off. But it was no use. So I just floated, too sore to swim, until the boat got close to me. I pulled myself up into the boat and requested a beer.

Williams whipped me a beer again. He missed, and the beer exploded against a large boulder behind me.

"Nice job, you prematurely bald prick," I said. "The least you can do is throw me a fucking beer I can catch with my now-useless fingers. Look at my knuckles! That's blood!"

"Easy there, raft pro," Jimmy said. "I'll toss you a beer and also the emergency case. There's a joint in there, a lighter, and some Band-Aids. Fix yourself up; that shit had to hurt."

This calmed me down. I leaned back as much as I could and fired up the pinner.

The water had slowed down. Everyone was quiet now, relaxing and soaking up the beauty of nature.

The border is such a beautiful part of the country, and nobody knows about it. We watched the hills roll by, followed by large, flat valleys that swept in lustrous shades of orange and brown in every direction. There were patches of greenery here and there, but they weren't needed for aesthetic purposes. The orange and brown were doing just fine.

The river grew wider and slower as we floated down it effort-lessly, ignorant to time. We passed a few people on the Mexico side of the river every long while. We passed an old man walking with a donkey, and he looked just like that coffee guy. What was his name? Not Jose Cuervo, although he's good. Oh, well.

After another long while, entranced by the scenery and doo-bery, we came upon three small children walking along the bank of the river. They were splashing, playing, and fishing with cane poles—just having a blast.

I wanted to pull up beside them and yell, *Don't abandon your dreams!* But they wouldn't understand me, and they would probably whip me unconscious with their cane poles.

Eventually, the sun started getting low, and I knew it was time to start thinking about setting up camp somewhere. Personally, I was getting anxious to get off of the boat and start a fire. I was also hungry, seeing as how I had thrown up everything I had eaten since birth on the rapids.

After a while, we found a spot and paddled to shore. JB had

fallen asleep, and his big monkey arms were dangling over the side of the boat. This was a huge mistake on his part, as most young folks will tell you. Most of us were far too exhausted to jack with him.

But not Williams.

After we pulled our boats up onto the shore, Williams woke JB up by teabagging his forehead.

If you don't know what teabagging is, ask someone else; I don't want to get into it.

After JB calmed down from the disgusting view he had awakened to, we all got our packs out. We decided that we didn't need any tents, because the skies were so clear. We preferred to sleep under the stars whenever possible.

Devero began setting up the grill while Jimmy and JB tried to get a fire going. Williams and I got the steaks and beans (courtesy of Paisley Auto Group) out of one of our four ice chests.

Dinner was excellent. We ate five large rib eyes, grilled to bloody perfection, and a few cans of ranch-style beans.

At this point, we switched over to hard liquor in an effort to conserve our beer for the heat of the days. Three of our large ice chests were dedicated only to beer. There was water as well, but we kept it warm. You gotta have priorities.

"So when do you start your new job, Jim?" I asked him.

"Two weeks. I figure that gives me one whole week to clean out my system."

"Damn," I said. "I guess that's about when I'll be starting too. What are they going to pay you?"

"Forty grand my first year, with a chance to hit seventy-plus within a couple of years," he answered. "They're putting me in as a recruiter right away. They said that's rare."

I could tell Jimmy was preoccupied, thinking about something.

I could tell he wanted to start arguing about something again. I prepared myself.

"Legs, man," he began, "Tell me the truth. What really made you stop believing in God? I mean, all of these other guys believe in God. Over ninety percent of the globe believes in God. How could that many people be wrong?"

"I'm not saying they *are* wrong," I told him. "I'm saying I don't know. That ninety percent breaks up into a bunch of smaller percentages with different gods. Many of them are as old as the Christian God—some newer, some older. And each one of those gods says that all of the other percentages outside their own are going to Hell."

I took a long sip of whiskey.

"Are you telling me that if you'd been born in Afghanistan like Devero, you would be a Christian? No, you would be a Muslim. If you'd been born in Tibet, you might be a Buddhist. In Israel, you might have been a Jew. So, do you see a pattern here? Religion is in direct correlation with geography. Whether you are going to hell or not depends on where you were born. I just don't think any god worth following would be that cruel."

I paused slightly. "Part of me thinks that a god who demands worship is a vain god," I continued. "It hurts to say that, but let's get it out there. If there is a god, I just think it's an unimaginable one, totally outside of our range of thinking. How can anyone be sure they got it right? It's just not possible."

"We call that faith," Jimmy replied. "And of those percentages I mentioned, a large portion are some form of Christianity. I just can't imagine how empty it must feel to not believe in God. You don't have to take the Bible at its literal word, as long as you believe the message. You can't deny that the message is strong. And you have to see the power in a man giving his life so that we could all be saved. He showed us how to live a moral life. What do you have to lose by believing in God and going to church now and then? If you're wrong, nothing changes."

"Yeah, but you're equating religion with morality," I countered. "Should getting into Heaven be the reason you lead a moral life? No. That would be insincere. You should lead a moral life because it's the right thing to do, not because of a prize at the end. And I'm not saying Jesus didn't exist. He very well might have, and if he did, he was most likely a very good person. We could all learn some lessons from him. But was he a deity who could literally walk on water? That's a big leap."

I coughed.

"If I have to explain why I'm skeptical about God, I want to hear you explain the dinosaurs. The Bible starts at the beginning of the universe and ends roughly two thousand years ago. I've read the Bible, and let me tell you, there aren't any dinosaurs in there. And from the museum reconstructions I've seen, they would have been hard to miss."

"Well that's because you're looking at it from a fundamentalist viewpoint," Jimmy said. "I believe evolution most likely happened. Those first few days of creation could have been millions of years; I don't know God's clock. We're not all crazy Bible thumpers. You can't tell me that's not a rational explanation. Shit, man, how can you be a Republican and not be a Christian?"

"How can you be a Democrat and believe in God?" Williams shot back, right on cue. "Democrats are the last people that come to mind when I think of morality. They dedicate their souls to making sure every hooker has multiple abortions while having gay sex on a wildlife preserve. How can you align yourself with that party and preach morality at the same time?"

"He's got a point," Devero jumped in. "I can't picture Jesus blessing many hookers or abortion doctors. I never heard Jesus talk about gay sex, though . . . that's just Williams, so read into that psychology however you'd like, but I can't really imagine Jesus being pro-choice."

"You guys are so ass-backward," Jimmy said. "That's exactly who Jesus hung out with: the dregs of society—the prostitutes, the tax collectors. He hung out with the poor. Your party has marketed Jesus as a businessman. Jesus was about helping people, and that's what Democrats are about. You guys think we should throw a single mother with three kids out on the street."

"No," Williams said, eyeballing Devero and Jim before returning to the topic. "We think she should get off of her lazy ass and get a job. Republicans think the lazy unemployed woman should stop having babies. If she's not in a wheelchair, there's no reason she can't hold down a nine-to-five. But you guys don't want her to get a job and provide a good example for her children; you want me to pay for her fat ass to sit around and eat Pop-Tarts and smoke menthols."

"I guess I'm to assume that the menthol cigarettes mean she's black," Jimmy half joked. "Is a brother gonna have to knock the shit out of you again?"

"Time for another joint," I said, trying to head off another fight. "Devero, do what you do best and please roll us a monster. Williams, it appears as though JB has fallen asleep again. I think another teabag is in order."

17

Alright, then, let's get to my spiritual upbringing, since it keeps coming up. This will probably be a helpful tool in letting you know how Brian "Legs" Hamilton came to be.

I was born into a Baptist family in Fort Worth, Texas, in 1974, right in the middle of the Bible Belt. Our church was close-knit, the kind where everyone went to worship once or twice a week before returning to their drinking and swearing grind.

The pastor was one of those charismatic, truly good through and through, inspirational people. He would end each service the same way, asking those who had not given their lives up to Jesus to hear the call and join him now.

Or burn in hell.

I became old enough to attend church camp the summer before first grade. I jumped at the opportunity. It was a wonderful camp, held in the deep woods of East Texas. Camp was a week long, filled with arts, crafts, swimming, and hiking. And every night was the revival.

Our pastor ended every night the way he ended every day of church. It was time for a close relationship with Jesus. At camp, I was one of the first to walk down that aisle.

I enjoyed the feeling so much that I walked down that aisle every summer until the seventh grade, at which point I was finally notified that once was enough. Once you buy the insurance, you're covered. Thanks for the news, six years later.

After the fourth grade, my parents transferred me from a Baptist school to a Church of Christ school, although I still continued to go to Baptist summer camp. The Church of Christ was a bit more fundamentalist than the Baptist Church, and my parents thought that was a good thing. Whereas at Baptist school and Baptist church, the congregants would worship and then return to "normal" lives, at the Church of Christ school and church, there was no "normal" life to return to.

It was like the town in *Footloose*. The final straw for me at this school was being thrown into detention for dancing, when I was merely skipping down the hall with my arms raised because I'd gotten a good grade on a test. But they said I was dancing, and, apparently, that's some pretty evil shit. True story. That actually happened in the late twentieth century. No bullshit. Dancing apparently ran parallel with attending an orgy at Lucifer's house on heroin.

After a couple of years at the School for Crusade Training, I decided I should make an early departure from the Church of Christ. My parents thought if the Baptist porridge was too cold, and the Church of Christ porridge was too hot, maybe Catholicism was the way to go.

"Let's get this kid in a Catholic school," they said. "It will be just right."

In preparation, I was sent to Catholic Church camp. Camp

TeCaKiCa—Texas Catholic Kids Camp. No bullshit. That was the name. It was at this camp, located on the Texas–Oklahoma border, where this culmination of things in my life—faith, developing skills as a smartass, and the bully factor—all . . . well . . . culminated.

This is a true story, and a poignant one at that: All of the future eighth graders were riding horses. One camper per horse, two horses in the corral at a time.

One of the more redneck/ass-backward fellows whom I didn't particularly care for was dismounting his horse, and his foot got caught in the stirrup. This flipped him upside-down beside the horse, and he landed face-first in a steaming, wet pile of horseshit.

I figured anyone could clearly see the comedy in the situation, so I laughed. It wasn't a mild, subdued laugh, mind you, but more one from the gut that just wouldn't stop. It was what one might call a throaty laugh.

In comes the bully.

The bully, in this case, aside from me and my laughing, was a young gent who looked like Frank Poncherello from *CHiPS*, in full Western attire and wearing the badge of a camp counselor. He asked me what I thought was so funny.

On the talk show in my head, I had plenty of hilarious answers, but I couldn't use any of them.

He then beckoned a ranch hand to bring out the oldest, largest, most ill-tempered horse in the stable for my personal riding pleasure. His exact words, painstakingly chosen, were "Bring out Jake." That short sentence had the effectiveness of that scene in *Pulp Fiction* where Zed says, "Bring out the gimp."

I do not profess to be a master of anything, really. Especially not horses. No equestrian will ever look to me for advice. But I have got a good grip on the obvious. The obvious was this: Jake was much larger than the other horses.

So the current bully in my life decided it was an excellent idea as retribution for my laughter that I should ride a horse that had been previously stabled for his temper.

When I mounted up, Buckaroo Asshole smacked the ass of this horse so hard that a gentle ride was now out of the question.

At the top of his voice, Buckaroo Asshole then shouted, "*Yaah!*" And so the ride began.

In the corral, I noticed Lee Hickter coming up fast behind me on his own horse. Lee got right in that zone that folks like Buckaroo Asshole tell you you're not supposed to get in, riding far too close to the horse in front of you. As the horses increased their speed, I noticed that Lee's horse's head was quite possibly entering my horse's ass.

And then it happened.

I've since been told by witnesses of the incident that I may have had a career in full-out rodeo riding. If I didn't hate horses, I might've given it some thought.

The horses began to fight.

Don't get me wrong; my money was on Jake. I just wanted a different seat for the fight.

Lee got a different seat pretty early on. He lacked the kung fu grip I had, I guess. He should've masturbated more often to improve his hand strength, as it appeared to be finally working in my favor. Lee flew a good fifteen feet before landing and screamed like a four-year-old girl as he ran back to Buckaroo Asshole, who was at this time contemplating an error in judgment on his part.

You would think that someone might jump in and help a kid in this situation, but I guess camp counselors aren't compensated very well for their duties. For the first time in my life, I got to experience that warm feeling of being expendable. But I was also in this Zen-like state of bronco riding.

I decided to wait for the proper time to jump and run. That time never presented itself, though, so I just jumped. I cleared Lee's total distance thrown while still on the upward arc.

When I landed, Jake and I locked eyes, and he made a break for me.

I ran like an extremely fast sissy, as is my style, all the way to the stupid-looking six-foot ranch fence and jumped right to the top of it—abruptly falling to the other side.

For a moment, I thought the fence had obtained ownership of my ballsack.

There, I was greeted by a now-laughing Buckaroo Asshole, who told me an old line that I have never looked at the same way since: "You know"—he paused to spit a big wad of chewing tobacco into the dirt—"you fall off a horse, you gotta get back up on him and ride again."

"Fuck that, cowboy!" I said. "That bastard needs to be Elmer's Glue or a Chinese entrée by sunrise!"

When Buckaroo Asshole went to grab Jake's reins, Jake reared up on his back legs. He turned sideways, fell, and rolled right on top of him. The asshole didn't break any bones, but he did have to spend a few days in the camp's infirmary—which I know because I got the bed next to him while I was playing sick to get out of horse riding the following day.

"What are you doing here?" I asked him. "You gotta get back up on that horse and ride!"

I truly believe he would have killed me if he had been able to stand.

18

I had begun attending an Assembly of God church with some friends by the time my high school years had started. I was completely in awe of that place. People speaking in tongues were not something I was accustomed to, and I feared that snake handling was just around the corner.

And with the new church came the obligatory new church camp. This particular church camp was on South Padre Island, where we partied all day and tried to interpret the tongues at night. It was kind of like Billy Graham on acid. I loved the people in that church, especially the pastor's kids, because they partied their asses off, but the Power of the Spirit seemed to work differently in me than in them.

They would raise their arms and wave their hands (which they referred to as "antennas to the Lord"), screaming and yelling in tongues. I tried a few times to speak in tongues, but things just didn't work like that for me. I was just yelling random things like I had Tourette's or something.

Not that anyone else noticed.

Anyway, I could feel that my own personal religious experience was starting to become tainted. For instance, my Catholic school bordered, in my opinion, on Communism. We had strict hair guidelines, and we had to wear the exact same uniforms bought at the exact same place.

For a smartass struggling to be unique, it was a blow to the system. I wore a shirt to school one day that was virtually the same as all of the other kids' shirts but had a little horse logo. The teacher, Brother Something-or-other, drew attention to this detail in front of the entire class. He told me that wearing that shirt was part of an effort on my part to make other students feel inferior and that I should be punished. No bullshit.

So the next day, I wore a similar shirt with a similar horse, only this time I pinned a little sign next to it that read, *This is not an effort to make you feel inferior.* Needless to say, that went over like Planned Parenthood at a pro-life rally, and I ended up in detention.

That teacher went on to become principal the year after I graduated. Not too long after his promotion, he was arrested in a local park for trying to pick up a friendly neighborhood male undercover officer for a BJ. He made national news.

So, in the larger scope of things, it turns out the horse on the shirt was pretty inconsequential.

But this school was hard on me. While I was still on a spiritual journey, I was also coming to grips with how ridiculously skinny I was. I was far from a stud with the ladies. Most girls wanted a more chiseled dude. So I guess I tried to do anything I could to keep my mind off the fact that I was a malnourished-looking, spiritually lost kid with a growing disrespect for authority, and I began to question not just my religion but religion itself. I went off the path of righteousness—way off. But sometimes you have to take the long way, or the wrong way, to get to the right place.

I can remember the first time I questioned the Bible. It was in my freshman-year religion class. Our teacher, Mr. Wooten (in hindsight, a total pothead), decided to let us in on some discrepancies in the Bible.

You see, up until this point, I would have laughed at someone for believing in evolution. I would have discounted them as a mindless idiot. Science and proof and fact be damned; the world was created in six days, and God rested on the seventh, so shut the hell up. You don't know what you're talking about. I do.

First, Mr. Wooten told us that, when the Bible was translated long ago, the Red Sea was used as a translation when it should have been the Reed Sea. The Reed Sea was a swamp not too far away from the Red Sea. You can walk right through a swamp if you need to. It's no miracle. He then said that the word "virgin" meant "young lady" back when Mary got knocked up. It makes you think. So, I thought, if some of the translations were wrong, well . . . Six days seems like a pretty good finish time on a universe.

It was at about this time that my church-shopping days ended and my days of being a heathen began. I became a talented vandal, miscreant, and party machine. The funny thing is that many of my best friends were made during that time period, and they all traveled the dark, fun, winding road with with me.

I was the first to wake up the next morning. I slept in the boat, but what I found back at the fire was pretty amusing.

Devero was facedown in the dirt, nowhere near his sleeping bag.

JB was faceup, spread-eagle, wearing only his tighty-whities. He was at least pretty close to his sleeping bag. JB was also experiencing a case of morning wood. It was horrifying.

But not as horrifying as Williams.

Williams still sat in his folding chair, which he'd never moved from the night before. His head was cocked to the side with his mouth open, and he was drooling. He was still balancing a warm glass of whiskey in his hand.

Well . . . in *one* hand.

In the other hand, Williams was holding his reasonably small, flaccid penis. The fact that his shirt was on the ground beside him and his underwear was around his ankles suggested that either it might not have been flaccid just hours before or he might have fallen asleep while trying to wake it up. Either way, as much as it scarred my retinas to look, I had sensory overload with such an incredible variety of ways to really effectively fuck with the guy that I couldn't look away. We had to get him. Really damn soon.

In stark contrast to the rest of the crew, Jimmy was the only one to successfully manage to get into his sleeping bag.

I looked back at Williams again. My mind was racing. I knew Williams generally popped a pill before sleeping and that he was an extremely deep sleeper. We had drawn on him a million times with permanent markers as he slept. But this called for more than mere magic markers. He had never passed out mid-whack in a lawn chair on a riverbank before. I would bet that not many people had.

We had to immortalize this on film. I grabbed the Polaroid camera from the Q boat and then quietly woke up the other guys. I could tell that the presence of a naked, penis-clutching Williams disturbed them as much as me. But, like me, they couldn't *not* look. We all huddled up.

"Guys," I said, "what can we do here to really shut his ass down for good? I have the camera. I think we all need to pose with him."

"Dude—JB," Devero said. "You have a boner."

"Ignore it," JB responded.

"Dude, I can't ignore it," Devero insisted. "You're sitting right next to me in fucking Fruit of the Looms. I can't even think about you having a boner next to a naked Williams. Something's not right with that. Please just do something."

"Fine," JB said, starting to pull on a pair of shorts. Then, as his zipper neared the top on its way up, he froze solid for a moment. He looked up at us with wide eyes.

"Guys, wait!" he exclaimed. "I've got it! Give me the camera!"

I handed it over and then looked on in horror as he moved close beside Williams, dropped his pants, stood with his johnson less than two inches from Williams's open, drooling mouth, and snapped a picture. He conveniently didn't include his own face. Then he snapped about five more.

It was disturbing on *so* many levels, but it was funny as hell.

Neither Devero, Jimmy, nor myself were willing to do what JB had just done. He deserved accolades for his work, but we just couldn't make that commitment.

But we weren't going to let him have all the fun. We pulled one ice chest right up behind Williams's lawn chair, and we pulled the others up on each side. Jimmy stood on the ice chest behind Williams while Devero and I stood on the ones on the sides. We all faced away from Williams.

"You ready?" I asked JB, who was standing several feet in front of us with the camera.

"Okay, guys . . . Drop 'em!"

Three pairs of shorts hit the ground, and Devero and I backed our bare asses up to the sides of Williams's face and squished his cheeks like kids do in preschool—except we were pushing much, much harder, and with our asses, not our hands.

Then, the cherry on top that completed the Pyramid of Asses: With our ass-cheeks holding Williams's face upright, Jim sat his bare ass right on top of Williams's mostly bald head. He pushed down pretty hard. Williams was pretty much wearing Jim's ass as a hat. I believe Jim may have farted also. Actually, I'm sure of it.

We used up all of the film for the whole trip right then and there.

Then we locked away the Polaroid and the pictures, and we all lay back down and pretended to be asleep.

Eventually, we got bored. I threw a rock at Williams's back really hard, so he'd wake up. My aim sucked, and it hit him in the head—but he started to rouse.

I could tell he'd awakened by the rather impressive fart he let go just a moment later. It had a great baritone sound to it and probably went on for six or seven seconds.

I could hear him whisper, "Aw, fuck yeah . . ." when the fart was over.

Then he obviously realized that he'd passed out while flicking the bishop, because we could hear some really frantic rustling around.

"Wake up, douchebags!" he yelled after a minute. "Jesus, do you guys just sleep all day? I've been up forever. Let's get some grub rolling!"

We all pretended to wake up, with the full knowledge that at some point in the next few minutes, hours, or days, those photos would come back to haunt him. It took a good half hour before any of us could even make eye contact with each other without almost cracking up.

I got the fire going so we could cook up some oatmeal and coffee. We had a big day ahead of us. I got out the waterproof map and analyzed it. We would be going over a few sections of pretty hairy rapids today. Today would be one of those days where people who did this often would probably wear helmets. *Pussies*.

If we made good time, we would enter the canyon early tomorrow. The canyon was supposed to be amazing. Supposedly, famous outlaws such as Billy the Kid had hidden out in the canyon, using some of the many caves hidden among its walls. We would remain in this rarely traveled canyon until the last day. Our pick-up point was a few miles past it.

But that was tomorrow. Today was going to be a bitch. Not like the day *after* tomorrow, which would end with the heaviest shit we'd see out here, but it was still gonna be a bitch.

And thank god I was no longer manning the Q boat. We had

already decided that JB would do his turn last, and I had already served, so that only left three candidates. And we all know how we solve a three-way tie.

Williams was the odd man out. Oh, sweet justice.

We finished our coffee over the glorious sound of Williams's bitching. I showed him the map, pointing out where the rough patches would be. We slowly gathered our shit, which had, by now, been spread out over a large section of real estate. Finally, after we had packed away our backpacks and ice chests, we took our positions in the boats.

We then cracked our first beers of the day. There was no need to wait. And my god! What a wondrous sound that cracking noise was in this setting! That was surely the nectar of the gods.

"Hey, Williams," I said, "is that a water moccasin coming up behind you?" I really didn't think he would look, but I was glad he did.

I hit him square in the face with an oversized mossball as he was turning back around to ask what I was talking about.

Just as I had suspected, this boat was more fun.

Hopefully, Williams could provide us with the same kind of fun manning the Q boat that I had provided yesterday. I would do my part to help. I didn't want him to get hurt, but I definitely wanted him to fall overboard.

To help him cope with his new responsibility, Williams thought it would be a good idea to eat some mushrooms. I completely disagreed with him, but he just kept popping them in his mouth. JB decided to join him. The rest of us decided to wait until at least after noon.

For the first hour, we just drifted. Then the water started picking up speed. Williams and JB were living in a completely different solar system. They kept making faces at each other and throwing shit. Sometimes they would just stare at each other, motionless.

"Okay, guys, life jackets on," I said. "The rapids are coming up soon. This is going to be a big section of class 3s and 4s. And whatever the fuck that bastard Jorge said had something to do with these rapids being wild."

We all looked ahead and saw the first drop. It was followed by a series of many other drops, and I began to wonder what the hell Williams was going to do.

"Jorge's on the gunship!" Williams screamed. "He's leading us to the donkey show!"

"*Yahoo-oo!*" JB yelled back. "Follow that little bastard!"

Okay, they were gone. Completely.

"Look at all the fish!" JB screamed. "They're everywhere! That's amazing! We've gotta catch some!"

There were no fish.

As we came up on the rapids, Williams managed to keep his ship straight. In fact, he went over the first section flawlessly. He was in the zone. Maybe everything was going to be okay.

Then he slammed the left side of his boat against a rock and turned completely backward, facing us.

"How the hell did you guys get in front of me?" Williams yelled. "Jesus, did you jump over my boat or what? Turn around!"

Wow. He was really fucked-up. He didn't even turn around; he still thought he was going forward. If he had turned around, he would have seen the big rock at the top of the second section of rapids.

But he didn't. He hit it solid and flew over the back of the raft and out of the boat, his head narrowly missing the rock. I had gotten one of my wishes.

The other wish was that he would be alive for this, and that was yet to be determined. We couldn't see him anymore, but we kept hearing his "*yaaaaaa-hoo!*" every few seconds. JB was ghostly white, thinking he had just lost the only one he had a "connection" with.

The Q boat remained upright behind us. It was running into shit pretty hard, but it wasn't flipping.

"There he is!" JB exclaimed. "Over there!"

"That's a log," Devero said.

"No, over there!" JB screamed again. "What's that climbing up on that rock?"

"There's nothing climbing up on that rock," Jimmy replied.

Just then, we saw Williams go over the third section of rapids. He was hauling ass. And laughing. He was having far too much fun to realize how close to death he was.

We were in a section of the river that boasted not only many drop-offs but many turns as well. And Williams had gone around those turns before us. We'd lost him.

JB was panicking, trying to come to grips with the realization that we might never again hear Williams's bigoted, sociopathic rants again. Minutes passed that seemed like hours, and as JB slipped into shock, the silence cut like a knife.

We went over the final set of rapids with difficulty, knowing that Williams's chances of surviving such mayhem without the protection of a raft were fading fast.

JB loaded the flare gun and shot a round directly into the water, after which he was tackled by Jimmy and disarmed.

Then, as we came around the next turn, we spotted Williams. He was clinging to a rock in the middle of the river, shaking and looking distraught, beer in hand. As we neared his rock of salvation, he looked at us like a newborn who had just emerged from the womb.

"Fuck, those mushrooms are strong," he said.

"No shit," replied JB. "And those fucking flares are useless."

"Don't worry about me, guys, I'll catch the Q boat," Williams said, as it was quickly approaching. It looked like his idea was to jump into it as it passed.

He made an Olympic leap toward the unmanned boat, bouncing gracefully off the back end and back into the river. He managed to catch the boat shortly after and pulled himself aboard and into the driver's seat—amazingly, still clutching his beer. He then chugged the beer, which was no doubt about 99.7 percent river water, and crushed the can against his head, discarding the empty can into the river.

"C'mon, dipshit," Jimmy shouted at him, "you were just saved by the grace of God, and now you're gonna throw a beer can in the river? What kind of hippy are you?"

"Take it easy, Afro Man," Williams called back. "We're all failed hippies. Get a grip on that and hook a brother up with a fresh brew."

That fresh brew hit him square in the chest. Hard. Wisely, he said nothing about it.

Williams sure had a way with words. Shit that was funny when other people said it just sounded fucking awful when he said it. "Afro Man."

At some point, Jimmy would surely kill him. I thought for sure that, as we tied our boats together, Jimmy would swing the anchor at him. Somehow, he managed not to.

But Williams did have *one* good point, which was a rarity. We were all failed hippies. We wanted to be hippies, sure. We loved the Grateful Dead. We couldn't resist the bonding power of hallucinogens. I mean, we certainly really felt a connection to the general philosophy. But I, for one, just couldn't adhere to all of the rules. I was a conflicted man: Sometimes I just wanted to throw away my beer bottle without recycling it. Not in a river, mind you, but you get the point.

And I had to shower twice a day—current circumstances with-held, of course.

Oh, I also liked my women shaved. You know, hit the pits and legs with a Gillette from time to time, and take a little off that other spot as well. Was that really too much to ask?

And what about employment? Hippies didn't believe in the con-cept. They believed in the power of love. The power of love was great and all, but it sure as shit wouldn't buy you a sandwich and make you smell good.

"I am a failed hippie, guys. We all are. Williams is right about that." I said this much like an alcoholic admitting his problem.

"But at least Williams has had success as a racist," Jimmy added.

"Aw, shit, here we go again," Williams said, exasperated. "I'm not a racist; I just call it like it is. That's one big reason I could never be a hippie: I look at the world through the eyes of realism. I know that drives you crazy, Jim. I'm sure it's a hard pill to swallow, that your race makes up the overwhelming majority of the criminals in this country. You are the exception to the rule, and you should be proud that the choices you've made haven't given you eight babies on welfare and a prison sentence."

"My Lord" was all Jimmy could say.

"Look, man, a large portion of your folks are in some stage of the penal system. Seventy percent are born into single-parent families. Most folks in Africa are on their way to full-blown AIDS. And I didn't do it; it's the choices that black people make. And they keep making them. And what do they offer as a solution? Handouts. Why should I hand someone money out of my pocket when they'll take it straight to the crack dealer? It's an endless cycle. And pointing that out is supposed to affirm my position as a racist?" Williams spewed proudly.

"Absolutely," Jimmy replied calmly, without hesitation.

Wow. I don't think any of us saw this coming. We were witnessing man at his lowest, in the form of a hallucinating silver spooner. This was no longer the jovial banter to which we had become accustomed.

"You are completely blind," Williams blared like a right-wing radio host. "You can't see what's really going on. Jesse Jackson has tainted your mind. And you are totally fucking up my mushrooms."

"Years of inbreeding have tainted *your* mind," Jimmy retorted. "Ignorant assholes like you only perpetuate the problems and enhance them. Jesus, are you completely incapable of seeing what the effects of something so horrible as slavery could be for a race? Do you really have no heart? Are you fucking with me right now? Because we all know you're an asshole, but . . . my god!"

Jimmy's fists were clenched tightly around the oars. His knuckles were turning white, the only sign of his increasing agitation.

"Slavery is over, Jim," Williams said, rolling his eyes. "It ended a long time ago. How about some personal responsibility? I don't own slaves and never have. You need to wake the hell up. All black people aren't bad—but a lot of them are. Have you ever considered that it might just be in the genetics? Seriously, dude!

"As humans evolved, it is not inconceivable that people's genetics were set to their surroundings. Maybe Asians are so smart because they evolved in areas where they had to find more creative ways to survive; the environment they evolved in required ingenuity as an only means to survival. Perhaps it was the same with white people. And black people, coming from Africa, were surrounded by jungles full of food and shelter, and they didn't have to think as much to survive. Their brains simply didn't need to evolve as much. Is that such a difficult concept? No. Does that mean that all black people are unintelligent? No. But I'm speaking in generalities."

Williams looked so proud of himself, as if his comments were somehow based on thorough anthropological research.

"So what you are saying is that some races *are* supreme," Jimmy replied. "Right on, man. White power. But under your theory, another problem arises. You have the issue of the evolution of the white man; that's the other side of this coin. If one race feels it reigns supreme over another, and over many years that so-called supreme race makes a habit of beating, killing, raping, and enslaving folks in an effort to remove the physical and mental workload from themselves, would that not cause the white man's brain to evolve toward a truly mean, lazy, and less intellectually capable composition? Under your hypothesis, does that mean that white people have become weak, stupid, and evil as a race?"

Jimmy laid down his oars and continued. "Now, I don't believe that for a second, and everyone on *this* boat is evidence of that being bullshit. But I've gotta say, this really makes me sick. You've revealed yourself, and it ain't pretty. You think the black race is a mongrel race, and no God I believe in would approve of what you are saying, much less grace you with any kind of pleasant afterlife. And if I thought for a moment that beating the shit out of you again would change your mind, I would do so gladly."

"Then maybe you're not so different from the others after all," Williams kept pressing. "Resorting to violence seems to be a theme among black people. That's how they get those fancy sneakers."

"Right, and slavery was a peaceful social institution," said Jimmy, shaking his head. "It's too bad that in your theory of the evolution of the white man's mind, you got skipped. You're a fucking idiot. You need help evolving."

"Maybe I can get the government to give me a handout," Williams replied in a shitty but quiet voice.

We all looked on in disbelief. I no longer understood how any of us had ever befriended Williams in the first place. But I think that's what happens when you get older: Sometimes people pull back the curtains and show you the strings.

I thought I would see anger in Jimmy's eyes, but I didn't. I saw sorrow and pity. I saw a man whose father and brother were killed not so long ago by a man with those same feelings, although those feelings had been worn a bit more on his sleeve in that case. But the ignorance Williams displayed that gets passed on from generation to generation seemed to be slowly crushing Jim inside, and it was heartbreaking to witness.

I felt lucky to have a friend like Jimmy. And I also felt that by forming a close association with Williams, I had somehow betrayed that friendship. And right now I was giving aid to Williams by staying silent, as we all were. Jim was twice the man Williams could ever be. Sometimes, I think we subconsciously associate ourselves with those who look like us. Like the way a white kid doesn't just go over and sit with the black kids at lunch and vice versa. And we let that continue.

Then maybe it becomes a situation where, for instance, when a couple of white guys get in a fight with a couple of black guys, spectators will jump in and join according to race, no matter who is right or wrong. But we can change the direction of these subconscious gestures. We can choose to jump in on the side of those who are right. And so I did.

"Fuck you, Williams. You're a piece of shit."

There, I said it.

The river widened again now, and the water had calmed. Williams settled back into his psychedelic experience, as did JB,
but now none of the rest of us felt like talking. I think the conversation we had just witnessed had taken a lot out of all of us. We were
forced awkwardly into reflection.

Or maybe it was the weed. It was pretty good weed, after all.

But lately, I'd been having a recurring thought: I didn't like the
guy I'd become. I decided that now was as good a time as any to start
exploring that, floating in this serenity that was coated with harsh
emotions, feeling a bit like some swift-boat guy in *Apocalypse Now*.

I was glad I'd stood up for Jim, though. You may not think that's
a big thing, but perhaps you can't appreciate my situation. You see,
I hadn't been in the habit of doing the right thing for some time.
And it had been weighing on me. I wasn't a serial killer, I didn't beat

people up for no reason, and I didn't antagonize the handicapped. But that didn't necessarily make me *good*.

And I guess that somehow it's a good thing when you can actually realize that you're not a good person. Because if you try, if you make those little decisions to be a little better here and there, then maybe, over time, you could actually achieve the status of "good person."

I was just glad I'd stepped in with *something* back there—some support for the guy who was being wronged. Jim would've done it for any of us, even Williams.

I used to be a bit of an ignorant bigot myself. This was due in no small part to other people around me, older people during my developmental years, who influenced me in the kind of decisions that could at first seem small yet over time form your character. It wasn't like I shaved my head and put on combat boots or got a swastika tattooed on my wrist. It was just the little things that trickled down that generational waterfall. Thankfully, my parents weren't responsible for any of that. But it found me, like it finds most stupid kids of any color.

I remember when I first realized I was an ignorant bigot. I mean, don't get me wrong—I had friends of all shades. But that something that trickled down had been engraved in the back of my brain long ago, and every now and then it just popped up. I had never really cared too much that it popped up here and there, either. I was somewhat unaware of it. It was just jokes—but not jokes I would tell in front of Jim. Jim and I joked about race, but this was different.

I guess maybe I thought that since Jimmy and I had become good friends, I had some kind of right to be a racist from time to time. I subconsciously felt like . . . perhaps I'd paid my dues to stamp out racism by becoming friends with a black guy, so I got a free pass.

You don't have to tell me how that sounds. It was a step backward, and it was short-lived. But it still happened.

Late in high school, Jimmy and I were driving to a party. We had been trying to get there for hours, but we kept getting caught up in other ordeals. So when we were finally able to break away and get into the car, we were a bit anxious. As I was turning to get on the entrance ramp to the expressway, a couple of black folks cut me off.

It just jumped out of my mouth. I had obviously been conditioned, much like when a secret service agent just leaps in front of the president; it's a trained reflex. Okay, maybe it's not that much like the secret service, but you get the picture. I won't say what I said at that moment, because you know what I said. It's a word I desire no ownership of, and it hasn't crossed my lips since.

But the look on Jimmy's face . . . I mean, god bless him. He did a great job of concealing the wound.

We exchanged fake smiles, and I gave a half-assed apology. But I couldn't help but think at that moment what an ignorant, bigoted shitbag I was for saying that.

And Jimmy . . . the look in his eyes behind this quasi smile he gave me. He was so disappointed. His mouth said, "No problem," but his eyes said, *Not you too! You've been a liar all this time!*

We never talked about it. I had been trying to compensate for that with him ever since.

"Jesus, Jim, come on, man. I was tripping my balls off. I was hardly in any state to fine-tune a point," I heard Williams explaining.

I didn't know how long I'd been passed out, but judging by how well I could read the words *I love hairy man ass* sunburned onto my chest through the clever use of sunblock, I'd been out for some time.

The sunblock tube was right beside Devero, so I suppose he was the one who had arranged for the message to be burned onto my protruding ribcage. And while it was hilarious, all eyes at this moment were transfixed on Williams as he tried to balance between apologizing and not admitting fault.

That was exactly what Jim was calling him on right now. "So, you're not wrong. You're not sorry. You're just misunderstood?" Jimmy said. "Poor little misunderstood bigot. Wow, man. I suppose I should apologize to you for not understanding your point about black people being an inferior race. My bad. Go on, now that your mind is free of its fungal cobwebs, go on and make your point for us again, won't you?"

"It all came out wrong, man. That wasn't what I meant," Williams backpedaled. "It's just that . . . You can't have a serious discussion about race nowadays without being labeled racist. Try to make a point, and here comes the goddamn liberal media, turning the facts around."

Jim gazed out into the distance for a moment before he spoke, locking eyes directly with Williams. "Dude, the reason I have labeled you a racist has nothing to do with the liberal media. The reason for it lies in your hypothesis concerning the formation of the brain in different races as affected by environment. Your conclusion— which you arrived at through strenuous testing, no doubt—was that the black race was less intellectually capable as a result if its surroundings in early years. Your argument continues onward to a conclusion that white people are more intellectually capable. In essence, according to you, whites are smarter than blacks. That, dipshit, is racism.

"If you want to have a serious discussion on race, I'm game," Jimmy continued. "But let's not insult ourselves with ideas borrowed from David Duke. Let's be real about it. And being real might mean that you have to come to some harsh realizations about what the white race has done throughout history.

"I won't deny that there is much crime in this country that is committed by blacks. And when we talk about a country the size of ours, that's big. But that's not where our units of measurement come to a close," Jim stated, as he proceeded to verbally hand Williams his ass. "It gets much bigger. Global. I'm talking about the Crusades, with white Christians trying their damnedest to wipe out yet another group of brown people, Arab Muslims. I'm talking about the mass murder of millions of Jews, due to what is basically an extension of your racial hypothesis, during the Holocaust. So we can look city to city, we can look state to state, or we can look at the world as a whole. Crack sales look pretty damned insignificant when stacked up against Auschwitz."

"That's your point?" Williams whined back. "Bad people in other countries? I'm talking about what's going on today, in my country. I'm talking about black people, at some point, holding themselves accountable for their station in life. Are you really *that* held back? Are you *that* oppressed?"

"My debate is about accountability as well," said Jimmy. "You deny that racism is an issue today, and I call bullshit. For instance, Legs and I went to the mall last week. We were both wearing tie-dyed T-shirts and shitty jeans, and everywhere we went, the store clerks watched us. And you might say, 'Yeah, that's because you looked like dirtbags'—and you might be right. But I went back to that mall after my job interview, wearing a damn nice suit and tie, and I went in some of the same stores, and I saw some of the same clerks. In a few of those stores, there were white guys, also wearing suits. And there were also some white guys in old T-shirts. But who do you think the clerks watched?"

"So you're basing your hypothesis on mall clerks?" Williams demanded. "How is that any better than mine? That's just petty bullshit. It's small. How can you actually be so weak as to let those jackasses affect you?"

"It's not weakness. It's disappointment. It's being let down by your fellow man," Jimmy replied.

"And it's not small," he continued. "It's everywhere. Everything we do, everywhere we go, in the back of people's minds, they've formed their own judgments, whether they're conscious of them or not. And these little things are passed on to their family and friends, in little words and in little actions, over time. It's like some intricately drawn, eye-teasing work of art. When you look at it from one angle, it looks like something harmless, yet when you turn it and approach it from a different angle, or in a different light, there is something large and new . . . something infinitely deep and dark. Having the vision to see the whole picture is not weakness at all."

"But what about choice?" Williams said. "Why do you think those mall clerks watch black people in their stores? Don't you think they have a reason? Of course they do. More black people have made the decision to steal from them than other races. You can't bring any socioeconomic bullshit to me when black people have a higher propensity to make the wrong choices."

"Who are you more likely to catch stealing?" Jim returned. "The person you're watching, or the person you're ignoring? And how can you totally disregard the socioeconomics surrounding the situation? Just because the game is the same for everyone doesn't mean that the teams are equal. A lot of the theft that occurs is out of necessity. If a guy doesn't have a job, and a bank won't give him a loan, how is that man supposed to feed his family?"

"If the theft is out of necessity, then it is forgivable," Williams said. "Wrong, but forgivable. But don't use that as a scapegoat. Look at the riots we saw in Los Angeles. We don't even need to touch on Rodney King. Look at the riots. Were all of those black people we saw on TV stealing bread? Water? Clothing? No, they were stealing big-screen televisions. How is a television a necessity for survival? And when they were done stealing these so-called necessities, they burned down the stores. All because they didn't get their way."

Jim put his face in the palm of his hand for a second, like you do when you realize that someone will never get it. Then he went in for another try.

"How can you bring up the LA riots but write off Rodney King as an inconsequential part of the equation?" said Jimmy. "That's the 'big picture' I'm talking about. Rodney King symbolized everything that's wrong with this 'level playing field.' The riots were the act of a people who had had enough. The rage had reached its limit. Yes, he was on drugs. Yes, he was resisting arrest. But does that excuse the cops beating him nearly to death with clubs? I mean, I know your conservative philosophy includes 'being tough on crime,' but does that entail having the holy shit beat out of you for breaking the law? No. And if your idea of restraining someone you've apprehended is clubbing them time and time again while they beg for mercy, then you should not be in law enforcement. You should be joining the criminals in prison. But you don't need to worry; it worked out for you. Those cops that nearly killed him all walked free."

Jimmy continued, somehow remaining calm. "As a black man in America, I understand that rage. I don't advocate for it. I wouldn't be a part of it if it came to my hometown. But I understand it, because as difficult as this concept is for you to understand, some people really never get a chance.

"There's a perpetual cycle that drags you down, and if you want to get out, too bad; you've made your choices already, so there's no second chance. If you go before a judge in the wrong zip code, there's a good chance that judge will think that, because of your zip code, you're beyond repair and must be kept off the streets to protect society. Then, after you've served your time, you're unemployable at any job worth a shit. So you're back to the same short list of bad options.

"*But not if you come from the right zip code.* If you come from the right zip code, that judge might look at you and think you're salvageable as a productive citizen. He might give you probation or drop the charges. And you might realize the mistakes you've made and make the most of your second chance.

"And you know what? When a society makes that subconscious decision that people from some zip codes are beyond repair, it's real hard for a person who lives in that zip code to not feel that. And instead of injecting capital into rebuilding those areas and being proactive, our society would rather inject that capital into the penal systems and be reactive. And so the cycle continues.

"That's what consumed those people in the riots. It wasn't Rodney King. It was the cycle. They had a short window of opportunity to let their voices be heard and their actions be seen. And, unfortunately, several chose violence and mayhem, which did nothing but reinforce the views of many white people.

"But if you listened really hard, there were plenty of people trying to tackle the issues the right way. Unfortunately, the burning buildings took up all of the network airtime, not the people fighting for progress," Jimmy finished, cracking a beer.

Damn, he was good. In that whole time, Jim's gaze never fell from Williams. Even when he grabbed his beer, he just reached back and found it without turning his head. His stare was solid.

This trip was turning into Jim's own LA riot. It was becoming a chance for him to look discrimination in the eye and go to battle. And while it was obvious that Jimmy was black and while we often joked about little shit and even debated lightly the subject of race, we'd never really viewed Jimmy as being any different from us.

Now I was beginning to look at him differently.

But before you think I'd taken a step back again, let me explain what I mean. I'm not saying I don't see color. People that say they don't see color are fucking morons. Of course we see color. Shut up. Please.

Different isn't always bad. I'm not trying to sound like a message you'd see in a *Highlights* magazine at your kid's dentist's office. I'm saying I was looking at Jim with new respect. We'd always just been stupid kids involved in stupid debates, but this was something very real to Jimmy, and that reality came across to all of us.

Well, almost all of us.

His speech to Williams had consumed Jim in a way I'd never seen. Maybe it was because of the pain of finding out that someone you thought was on your team is actually just visiting. The betrayal of a friend is a hard pill to swallow.

The thing that we saw in Jim was that he was fighting for something he *knew,* not something stupid and trivial (yet profound and complex) like we usually debated. He *knew* this. He *lived* this.

And while we had been aware, due in no small part to increased levels of darker pigment, that he was black . . . maybe we had been oblivious to what that sometimes entails.

Williams took the racial comfort zone that he delusionally thought he was a part of as an invitation to flaunt his views before Jim and the rest of us. He thought that because he had entered the same inner circle as a black guy, his thoughts must somehow have achieved some new level of credibility or justification.

"Jim, it's not that you don't make some good points . . ." Williams began again. "Because you do. But I can't believe that you buy into all that. I guess my point is, well . . . I thought you were smarter than that."

"Maybe I thought I was too," Jimmy answered. "Maybe, with all of my white friends, I thought that race didn't affect me. But when that guy killed my father and my brother, I found out that it did. They were just two more niggers to him. Two beautiful people: a hard-working, God-fearing, good man and his precious son, my brother . . . But they were just two more niggers. That's where the road you're on leads to, man. I pray that you'll recognize that."

Jimmy's eyes showed how deep his loss and sorrow ran and also how close to the surface it all still was. But hate was nowhere to be found.

And for the first time since meeting Williams, we saw him make the wise move of just shutting up.

24

And so we moped on down the river, with the two boats loosely tied together. The river had become wider and shallower a few miles back. Every now and then, we'd feel the boats scrape the bottom. It reminded me of Williams—shallow, wide, and hitting bottom.

There was definitely a dark mood setting in. Our last hurrah was becoming more negative than joyful. We were in the aftermath of an explosive argument that had revealed the unpleasant true colors of a close friend. It had pissed in our breakfast cereal. At times like these, one must take necessary actions to correct the direction of life. Redraw the map, if you will. Change the syllabus.

"Who's got the weed?" I asked.

"That would be me," said Devero.

"Rolling papers?"

"Me again, *mon capitaine*."

"I think that the current mood constitutes an undertaking of monumental proportions. I need something big."

"I'm on it, sir."

And so he was, like stink on a monkey.

I sometimes wondered whether Devero had gone through some sort of secret military joint-rolling training. Everything from the way he unrolled the bag to the way he placed the paper between his fingers, to the way he licked it with his tongue barely visible, to the one-handed twist finish, to the rerolling and storing of the bag . . . It was like watching a Marine break down and then reassemble a rifle. No matter how fast he went, he always rolled an immaculate joint.

This time, Devero rolled a joint so perfect that it was nothing less than a work of art. So finely crafted was this piece that Monet and Picasso would have easily been eclipsed by his artistry, had Devero been alive at that time.

"I call this work *Desegregation*," Devero said, holding his masterpiece aloft for us all to admire. "May it bring harmony to both boats, and may it bring some semblance of either reason or tact to Williams. We'll take either one."

My god, was this spliff big. After it made a few rounds, life gave signs of getting back to normal.

Williams stood up to pass the joint back to me on our boat. I was seated at the back, and Williams was trying to overcompensate with niceness. He knew he'd caused the current shitstorm, so he balanced along the side of his boat to hand it over, when normally he would've told us to kiss his ass. He even extended his arm and used the proper thumb-to-thumb technique.

Not a millisecond after I'd taken possession of the joint, our thumbs still barely touching, the boats scraped a shallow part again—a *really* shallow part, the kind that stops you immediately.

Williams and I never broke eye contact as he went sprinting

full-speed backward. It was like watching a video in rewind, or the "Near . . . Far" skit on *Sesame Street*.

He might have gotten some decent distance off the end of the boat if his ankle hadn't caught the rope on the edge. He stopped midair about two feet off of the end, like a dog running full-out and reaching the end of its chain, and then he dropped like a rock into about three inches of water.

Devero sprayed beer out his nose. JB fell backward laughing. I fell forward. Jim had the biggest grin I'd seen on anyone, possibly ever. JB even started laughing so hard that he threw up. We even heard a subdued *Beavis and Butthead* kind of laugh coming from the water.

Thank god, shit was fun again.

If world leaders could get together on a somewhat regular basis, sit in a circle, and just pass a friggin' joint around, there would never be a war again. As long as someone brought Doritos.

"Well, gang, it's time I leveled with you," I said when Williams was back in his boat. "I don't have a fucking clue what Jorge said about anything from this point forward.

"Actually, to be more accurate," I added. "I don't actually remember anything about Jorge. I'm not really sure the little fucker ever even existed. And so, in closing, I would like to say good luck to you guys over these next couple of days."

Man, I was wasted. I guess we had been drinking since the sun drove us from slumber. That monstrosity we referred to as a joint had driven us all nuttier than Chinese chicken salad. And I was starting to wonder if we should've been taking more safety precautions.

I wouldn't dream of bringing this up, for fear of exile—but none of us even had a life jacket on. Except Williams, who was a pussy.

That meant that if the boats ate shit, Darwinism was turned on its head. Only Williams would survive. The only thing we had gone great lengths to protect was the beer—so Williams would live and drink our beer. That pissed me off a little too: the thought of Williams spewing bigoted rants on the bank of the river, drinking our beer.

"Hey, Legs, man," Devero said. "Why do you look so pissed off? Are you freaking out, man? Do I need to get JB to fire off another flare?"

"I'm not pissed off," I replied. "Not losing it—not any more than you guys. No need to notify the authorities with JB's deft marksmanship. Just wondering if we should consider putting our life jackets on. That's all. The river might pick up. Jorge fucked us, remember?"

"Oh, I won't shoot a flare," JB said. "But I'm relatively sure that means you have a vagina. And I'm not talking about a small vagina. I'm talking *massive*. Like Williams's mom's vagina. Fucking huge."

"JB," I told him firmly, "I am going to crap on your chest while you sleep tonight. Do you guys realize what would happen if this boat were to capsize right now? Only Williams and the beer would make it. Williams would drink our beer."

This argument resonated.

"Oh . . . Damn. My bad, man; that would be awful," JB said. "He's right. We don't want Williams drinking our beer. Put your life jackets on."

"Hey, assholes," Williams piped up. "I don't know if you realize, but my boat is tied up to your boat right now. I'm right next to you. Give me a freakin' break, already. I was out of line earlier. I was shrooming, man, okay? I didn't mean to piss anybody off. Let's all just have a good time."

"Well, I'm sure that's as close to an apology as we'll get," Jimmy said, after a period of sustained silence. "You still need help, but we can move past that. Let's have a good time."

He leaned across the space between boats, and he and Williams clinked their cans together.

T he sun began to shift downward again. The beauty surrounding us was becoming all the more apparent. The quiet that we were now a part of was no longer due to suffocation from turmoil but, rather, a welcome state of serenity. We felt at one with nature, as if we could almost understand what the crickets were chirping about.

Eventually, we realized that the water was steadily speeding up. We tried to regain what little mental acuity that the weed, beer, liquor, and mushrooms left for us.

Once again we marched diligently into battle, with the currents and boulders proving worthy opponents. And again, showing our mighty intellect, we had cast aside our armor, which in this case took the form of life preservers.

Except for Williams, of course, who represented the constant vagina of our collective anatomy.

We pressed on through the rapids like seasoned veterans now.

The rapids were harsh, with tight windows to maneuver through, but we were in the zone. The river became so intense for a stretch that none of us made a sound, except the grunts and groans of massive physical exertion as we swung the oars wildly yet with precision. We struggled just to stay straight and upright as we whipped over drops and through turns.

I can honestly say we had not expected the river to get this rough. And this wasn't even the big stuff. The big stuff was still two days away. I didn't know if anyone else was having the same thought, but it had been bugging the shit out of me: I didn't know if we were capable of handling more.

But damn, we looked good. We were kicking ass. It came back to us like riding a bike.

Williams looked terrified, though, as he captained the Q boat through the last set. But, fucked-up as he was, he believed the lie he'd been telling himself that he was good enough to do this, and he prevailed. We emerged from the battle as victors, conquerors of nature.

The forward platoon and the secondary platoon tied up together on the other side of the war zone, and again we were one unit.

"Shit," Williams said. "I need a beer."

"I'm on it," said Jim, handing a beer across to him and showing a bit of mercy in not pointing out the trembling hand on the receiving end.

"What now, Captain?" JB asked me.

Captain? Was I the captain? Was I elected? Did I need to call for a recount?

"Okay . . . Devero, we need a large joint, stat," I replied, assuming the role. "And when I say big, I don't mean a circus freak. Maybe a King Edward. When you get done rolling it, put a flame on it. Then we'll start looking for a place to camp."

The adrenaline was flowing hard still as Devero went to work. I think we were all proud and surprised that we'd made it through this last bit untainted. I don't think any of us drank less than three beers in the five or so minutes it took Devero to craft another masterpiece. He did as instructed and put a flame to it. As we passed it around in our ritualistic manner, we scanned for a place to throw our sleeping bags and start a fire.

We were pulling our boats onto shore about halfway through the joint. The water moved slowly in this spot, and the river was wide. We had begun to stink a bit, so everyone stripped down to their underwear to relax in the water. We hoped this act might at least moderately wash the funk from our junk.

After rinsing off and peeing, submerging myself for what seemed like an eternity, I climbed ashore and began to make a fire. I let my friends marinate in my pee while I got the steaks ready.

After we were all done swimming and relaxing, we ate in exhausted silence and then reclined under the stars for our after-dinner whiskey.

"You guys know what I always think about?" Jimmy said. "I've been such a bastard in my life. In the back of my mind, I want to be this great person. I want to inspire people. But I can't get over some of the shit I've done."

"Like what?" Devero asked. "You're the saint of this group. What the hell have you ever done that's so bad?"

"Elton Ayers," Jimmy responded immediately. "We set that kid up to fail. He wanted to be just like us. He wanted to be one of us. Now he's paralyzed."

"Dude, that's not our fucking problem," Williams shot back. "It's not *your* problem. He was a dumbass. He probably still is."

"That's fucking cold, man," I said.

Elton Ayers was the tragically geeky kid brother of one of our fraternity brothers in college. He was about as skinny as me, but he had buckteeth and coke-bottle glasses. He was quiet and reserved. He made straight As and had no business being in a fraternity.

But he was a "legacy," meaning that his big brother was in the fraternity, so he was almost a shoo-in. Almost. In our fraternity's chapter meeting, when it came time to vote on whether or not to let him in, I had been the most outspoken against him.

I didn't want him in; he didn't belong. My argument was that he was a doofus and that we were cool—end of story. It was the best thing for him and us that he not join. My friends had agreed, but they had mostly kept quiet and let me do the talking.

It was unprecedented to not let a legacy in. Things got very heated, but I was adamant. I pissed off a lot of my fraternity brothers, as well as Bill Ayers, the kid's brother. In the end, I was overruled. Some of the brothers were so upset with me afterward that I was nearly thrown out of the fraternity for it.

Elton was given a bid, which he accepted with enthusiasm. During pledging, he kept trying his hardest to gain the acceptance of my group of friends. He had never had a drink of alcohol in his life before joining the fraternity, because his dad had died a severe and abusive alcoholic. But all that changed when he pledged.

Elton saw that my circle of friends partied pretty hard, and he wanted to be a part of that. He started showing up at our houses on acid, on mushrooms, on whatever he could get his hands on. He spent most of his waking hours trying to impress us. He even got a Jeep because JB had one.

We were nothing but cruel to him, but he would come back to us every time like a beaten spouse. We just *couldn't* let him in our group; he tarnished our image. But he kept coming back—more and more fucked-up each time.

Other guys in the fraternity were concerned and talked to him. They told him to stay away from us because we were bad influences. They asked us to talk to him, but we thought we had the high ground, because we never wanted him in the first place. They'd voted him in, so it was their problem.

A few months after initiation into the fraternity, Elton showed up at our door again. He was as messed up as anyone could be. He said he was tripping his balls off and had drunk a fifth of vodka. He said he needed a place to mellow out for a while. We had some girls over and were not entirely sober ourselves. We told him to fuck off and go home.

On his way home, Elton was going way too fast, enjoying the wind in his hair in his new Jeep. He ran through a red light doing close to ninety and clipped the tail of another car. The Jeep flipped numerous times, throwing Elton out. He broke his neck and would never walk or move his arms again. Some said he was lucky to be alive, but I'm not so sure about that.

The next day, when we found out, we barely remembered him coming by. Then we remembered what we did. Then it sank in. We had never talked about it, and we never told anyone what we had done. Elton didn't remember either, thank god. We had sort of shelved the whole thing until now.

"I never told you guys this," said Devero, "but when I was

delivering food last year, I delivered an order to his apartment. I didn't know it was him. The name didn't hit me until I saw him. I hadn't seen him since that night. He was all alone in this little apartment in his wheelchair, getting around with some joystick he used with his mouth. I talked to him for a little bit, told him I'd call him or come by again, but . . . I don't know. I couldn't even think about it. Fuck, man . . . We did that. All of us."

Devero had to quit talking, because his eyes were filling with tears. He was moving his mouth like he wanted to continue, but Jimmy rescued him.

"Bad things, man. We've done some really bad things. We should've put his ass in bed that night. I can't believe what we're capable of sometimes, you know . . . as people. We just let him go, and not a damned one of us ever went to see him after that. Dude ain't got nobody now, just his own lonely miserable-ass existence. I don't know how we sleep at night sometimes."

"On a comfortable pillow, that's how," Williams steamed. "It's not like we gave him acid and vodka and told him to take a drive. He did that on his own. Why do you let this shit bother you? It's sad, yeah. It sucks. But we didn't do it. You say he's alone *now*? He was *always* alone. Sad but true. I wish him the best, but I'm not going to sit here and pretend I put him in that wheelchair."

"So I guess you've never done anything you aren't proud of, Williams?" JB said. "I can't imagine how bad it must feel to be you. You're so fucking bitter, man. I can't understand where it all comes from."

Williams mumbled something about how this trip was supposed to be fun, and we were bringing the mood down, but we all kind of ignored him in disgust.

"How about you, Legs?" Jim asked. "What's your least proud moment?"

"Honestly?"

"No, lie to me, bitch." Jimmy smiled.

"Okay, well . . ." I took a deep breath. "Honestly, it would have to be when we were in high school, going to some party, and I dropped the N-word with you in the car. Maybe it sounds small; I don't know. It always stuck with me. You were my best friend, and here I was saying that shit. I never really even said I was sorry. When Darrell and your dad died, it was all I could think about. I thought you might see that bastard's face on mine a little bit. I hated myself for a long time when they died because I had said that. Same way you feel about Elton, I guess. It wasn't *me* who said the shit that guy said in court, just like it wasn't *you* who told Elton to get lost that night. But it *was* us. It was us at our lowest."

Jim just gave a half nod to this. I don't know, but I think that meant a lot to him. I hoped it did.

We all talked late into the night. It was somber but almost therapeutic. We all had some things we needed to say. And, except for Williams, we all said them.

I don't think any of us laughed at all that night, but it was good. It was good to have these people to talk to. And it wasn't bullshit talk. It was real. We didn't talk about things we thought we knew, like the usual shit, but we talked about things we actually knew. We talked about us.

The thing about Elton Ayers was that he had been part of a pattern. I hated to think about that, but it was true. He wasn't the first. I liked to bitch about the bullies, but I was that sonofabitch a couple of times as well.

It made me think about my freshman year in high school, a few years before tortured kids began taking up arms and executing their asshole oppressors along with the innocents. Obviously, killing people makes you garbage. But pushing people to even consider that makes you garbage too.

When my friends and I were freshmen in high school, we took in a new kid and let him join our group. We didn't do it because he was a cool guy or because he was a ladies' man or for any other justifiable reason. The simple fact was that none of us would get our driver's licenses for another year, and this guy had been held back a grade.

Eric was a good dude… He was just new. He was also the only true nonvirgin of the crew, although we all claimed to have mounted up on one unverifiable beauty or another. Most importantly, Eric had a car, so we would now have transportation in the form of an '87 Ford Escort.

I became better friends with him than anyone else did. We cruised for chicks, with limited success. We drank Strawberry Hill and smoked menthol cigarettes. He was always there for us, loyal and true.

I really don't know what went wrong, other than that, as time went on, we all began to get our own driver's licenses. His role in the group began to wane. Kids are just cruel sometimes.

Eric became the target of our sarcasm and the butt of our jokes. We started picking on him really for no reason. It was a shame, because he was probably a better person than any of us.

He slowly began to move outside of our circle, and as he did, we intensified our bullying. At the height of things, he got into one of those huge after-school fights, where the whole school circles around. Eric had never thrown a punch in his life. We all just stood there and watched while he got his ass very kicked. We even egged it on.

The very next day, I believe it was Williams who lobbed the burrito through Eric's sunroof, hitting him in the head. The burrito exploded throughout his vehicle. It seemed as though the whole school joined in to laugh at him . . . myself, unfortunately, included.

Eric vanished into obscurity after those days. Then one day, he was just gone.

He went to live with his father in some other state. His mother wouldn't tell us where, because she knew the kind of absolutely horrible people we'd been to him.

I began to feel guilty about what we'd done. How could I possibly have been so inhumane to a person who had done nothing other than be a friend to us? It tore me apart inside to think of what we put him through.

All that I know is that by surviving that time—by never lowering himself to our level, by getting up and dusting himself off after life just kicked the shit out of him—Eric was better than all of us. He moved out to Hollywood after high school and became a regular on a hit television series. He even got to play the lead villain in a somewhat major motion picture.

I am certain that he would be shocked to know how hard I rooted for him.

The reason I was rudely summoned from sleep the next morning wasn't the sun beating down on my face. It wasn't the jagged rocks I had unknowingly rolled over on in my drunken slumber, either. The reason was that Jimmy, who had been sleeping just a few feet away in his sleeping bag, was poking my forehead with a stick.

Just as I was about to scream, grab the stick, and whip him in the face with it, he made the *Shh!* motion with his finger to his lips and pointed to the tail end of the boat I had passed out in front of. I glanced over and saw yet another disturbing image that just might be frozen in my mind forever.

We had pulled the passenger boat about two-thirds of the way onto shore the previous night. The back end of the boat was in the water. It was there that Williams was performing a crude balancing act. He was holding the boat with one hand and had a copy of *Play-boy* in his other hand. His pants were around his ankles, and he was letting his ass hover just above the water while taking a dump.

Jimmy had obviously been witness to this gruesome sight long enough to devise a plan. He held up a roll of toilet paper that he had poured a bottle of water on——essentially making it a massive spitball.

"Time to play some honkeyball," Jimmy whispered.

Oh, shit.

Jimmy popped up, assumed a pitching stance, and flung the soggy roll at Williams, all in a fraction of a second. The great Nolan Ryan would have been impressed with his speed and accuracy.

Williams barely had time to glance up as it hit him square in the face, sending his feet over his head as he sailed backward into the water, landing atop a freshly dropped floater. The only thing that remained visible above the surface of the water was a *Playboy* subscription card, which sailed gently downstream.

"You son of a bitch!" screamed Williams as he burst through the surface of the water like Rambo. "It is *on*, man! It is *on!*"

"Mornin', sunshine," I said.

Everyone was awake at this point. Even Williams, emerging from the water, pulling his pants up from the front with his fat ass still hanging out the back, still clutching his soggy *Playboy* in his other hand, couldn't help but crack a smile.

He probably would've smiled less if he'd known that the turd he landed on stuck briefly between his shoulder blades on his T-shirt before dropping into the water. But he was smiling, so we didn't mention it, and we all made mental notes to not pat him on the back any time soon.

I think we all felt it then: This was going to be a good day.

We ate our oatmeal and loaded the rafts. JB decided to forgo his right to go last and volunteered to do his shift on the Q boat.

The river was supposed to be somewhat calm today. This was also the day we were supposed to enter the canyon.

We got our shit together quickly. We loaded the boats, and then we were on our way.

It wasn't long before the scenery started to change dramatically. The land on both sides of us began to grade steeply upward. The hue of our surroundings shifted from brown to green. The green had started at eye-level but quickly rose higher and higher. We were at the gates of the canyon.

It was breathtaking. The river was maybe forty feet wide now, with walls shooting toward the sky on each side that must have been two or three hundred feet high. The caves that surrounded us housed many memories of outlaws and bandits from days long past. In the canyon, we would have direct sunlight only when the sun was precisely overhead. The shadows all around us made the experience surreal.

"Devero, I think you know what this calls for," I said.

But he was already on it. He glanced up just to nod, and I nodded back. Good man, that Devero.

JB, our Q boatman for the day, had fallen behind us some time back, ignoring formation. We had to keep looking over our shoulders to make sure he was still with us. I was glad I had glanced back this time, because JB had fallen asleep, sprawled out on the ice chests, traveling backward. I quietly pointed this out to my fellow passengers.

"*Oh, fuck! Big fucking waterfall!*" Williams yelled, trying to make an ass of JB as he had been made an ass of himself this morning.

JB lay motionless, merely raising one ape arm and hand and extended his middle finger.

"Done," Devero said, in a low, monotone voice that was still loud enough to reach JB in the other boat.

All of us knew what that one word meant. Our group had achieved a higher level of communication, where one word conveyed the meaning of a group of sentences. It was a time-saving language method embraced by this band of intellectual heathens. The word *done* was interpreted by all as *I have completed the task of rolling a joint with precision craftsmanship using superb-quality marijuana. Please designate the proper locale where we may partake in its consumption.*

We directed the boats to a large cave nearby that opened onto the river at an angle, making it almost invisible to the eye. We paddled in.

The cave narrowed for twenty yards or so, then opened up into a much larger area, which was an underground lake roughly the size of a gymnasium, with a ceiling about thirty feet high. Our lanterns illuminated the entire cavern. We all looked around in stunned silence.

Canvassing the walls were stories told by painted pictures, articulated god knows how long ago by Native Americans.

That may not be correct, though, because we were on the southern wall of the canyon, which technically would be Mexico. So they were articulated by Native Mexicans.

But that doesn't sound right either. They must not have the whole "politically correct" thing in Mexico, because I've never heard of Native Mexicans when referring to the teepee/painted-face/casino crowd.

Fuck it. They were painted by Indians from Mexico.

Devero lit the joint while I passed around sandwiches. Williams took a rare turn at being useful, handing beers out to everyone.

This was *so* cool. The cavern appeared as if it had been untouched for eons. It was like being in a time machine.

"This is just mesmerizing, man," Jimmy murmured, taking a long inhale from the doob while staring at the paintings. "I wonder what all this shit means."

"You see that right there, Jim?" Williams said, pointing toward a painting behind him.

"That?"

"Yeah," Williams answered. "You know what that means?"

"No."

"It means pass the joint."

"Oh, because I thought it looked like a buffalo humping your great-grandmother."

"No, her hand is extended outward; she's definitely wanting someone to pass the joint."

"I don't think so. I think she's motioning to another buffalo. I think she wants to be double-teamed."

"She wants the joint. I'm positive."

Jimmy passed the joint.

"Man, I almost don't want to tell anyone we saw this," Devero said. "You know someone's gonna come in someday and mess this all up. They'll put a gift shop out front and sell Jet Ski rides inside. They'll give you a brochure and your own set of paints so you can add your own picture."

We all felt the same way. The beauty and history laid out before us could easily be cheapened and wiped away by the corruption of man. Isolation was the only protection for sites such as this.

But then I wondered if, before these Indians had painted on the walls, other Indians had come in and said, *Wow, this sure is pretty. I hope a bunch of Indians don't come in here and paint shit all over the walls.*

"Yeah, well, this is a capitalist country," Williams shot back. "You went to business school. There's nothing wrong with making a buck. Maybe you should head out to the Middle East. Afghanistan has plenty of caves. You could live in one if you want."

"Ayn Rand doesn't apply in all cases, jackass," Devero replied.

"Please, God, for the sake of all that is holy, could we please not argue about capitalism right now in this setting?" Jimmy said. "Besides, man, asking Williams to debate intelligently is like asking a dude in a wheelchair to take the stairs."

We finished eating and smoking in the cave and rowed out toward the light, baked to the core.

"Hey, JB," Devero called out as we neared the exit.

"What up, dog?" he replied.

"Doesn't this remind you of being born? You know, sailing out that huge hole without touching the walls?"

"Dude, your mom is so dirty I called her for phone sex and got an ear infection," JB deadpanned.

"Dude, your mom is so dirty she pours saltwater down her pants to keep the crabs fresh."

"Your mom's so dirty she got fired from the sperm bank for drinking on the job."

"Yeah? Your mom's so dirty even dogs won't sniff her crotch."

We carried on like this for a good half hour. Ancient caves notwithstanding, there are not many things in this life more sacred than "your mom" jokes. Our mothers would be so proud.

30

This was turning out to be one of the greatest days ever. We were well into the beer by midafternoon. We were having a blast, just laughing and taking it all in.

Then, in a masterstroke of Mother Nature, the sun broke into the canyon. We had been in the shadows of the canyon for hours, and when the beams from Heaven finally graced the river, it was magnificent.

Starting from the top of the canyon wall, the rocks began turning from dark brown to almost white. It looked like someone was pouring a huge bucket of sunlight-colored paint down the wall, until it was covered in it, and then it bled out into the water.

The beauty of it all was too much. We all immediately dove from the boats and began to bask in the rays.

Ironically, in this, the calmest section of the river we had seen, we all had our life jackets on. But not out of safety, mind you; this was due to laziness and inebriation. We wanted to float motionless for as long as possible, riding the fine line between mellow and unconscious.

Had you looked down into the river from above, you might have thought that there had been a terrible rafting accident—that there were five dead bodies just floating along. We looked like debris.

I imagined that even astronauts hadn't felt the same level of weightlessness that we felt now. Plus, we were one up on the astronauts, because we didn't have to wear space suits, which allowed us to drink beer.

The pull of gravity on the water was imperceptibly slow, and the arms of serenity cradled us in the sunlight.

At one point, I kind of jolted, like when you've just begun to fall asleep but your body screams at you and says, *Hey! Not so fast!* I raised my head and looked around, just as the sun disappeared across the other canyon wall.

How long had we been floating? How long would we still have sunlight? Five minutes? No. Fifteen? Maybe. An hour? It was possible.

I saw all of my compadres scattered around me in the water.

What I didn't see were the boats.

Everyone glanced downriver at about the same time and noticed that the boats had made some decent headway on us during our unquantifiable moment of experiencing some serious *one with nature* shit. This startled us a bit.

And I must admit it was a major letdown. We knew that reacquiring the boats would take something we really didn't want to give: effort.

Like most folks of our generation, the simple thought of giving effort to something (that didn't fall into a few very specific categories) absolutely disgusted us. This was like *really* getting into watching a movie, and right at the end, some jackass (usually a family member) asks you a question right when someone in the movie says something pivotal and profound that ties it all together.

This was exactly like that. Well, except that you could die from this if you went over the falls before you got to the boat. Other than that, it was identical, virtually a Xerox.

We all swam vigorously to close the distance between ourselves and the boats. They had about a two-hundred-yard head start on us. It took a long-ass time before we could tell that we were making any headway at all.

You could tell that we all wanted to make a race of it a few times. Each time we would make it for about ten seconds of "everything you've got," and then we'd have nothing.

As I pushed my drunken body to the limit, needles and knives of pain drove through my underdeveloped muscles.

Eventually, we made it. Everyone collapsed on the floors of the boats after using everything left to excruciatingly pull ourselves aboard. How long had we been swimming toward the boats? Five minutes? No. Fifteen? Maybe. An hour? It's possible. I lay on my back, staring at the dimming sunlight, and was overcome with the pleading of my body to let it reenter a supreme state of relaxation.

As I became enveloped by that state, a horrendous noise tore through the quiet from the bough of the Q boat, like a chainsaw through a buffalo's ass. JB was snoring. Seeing as how his snoring allowed only himself to sleep, and the boats were tied together, Williams climbed aboard and teabagged him. The snoring stopped.

There had been many times in my short life in which I had reached extended, supreme levels of relaxation. Sure, most had been chemically induced, but who's keeping score? The point is, I was an expert at relaxation. And *this* day, without question, had been the most relaxing day I could ever recall. But then we have the issue of what I could actually recall, due to the previously mentioned chemical induction. I was calm, okay? I was Valium in human form.

The only problem with such sustained periods of calm is that eventually the yawns sneak up on you. And they came upon us that day with a great vengeance. Mellow is cool. Tired sucks ass.

"Any ideas on how to wake our asses up?" I asked. "And Williams, don't say blow. You're the only coke-monkey here. We need to liven up, man. We've gotta keep on truckin' for at least another hour or two before we stop to sleep on the roses."

"Well, we do have more mushrooms," Williams replied. "I'm just sayin'."

I almost felt like documenting the time and place of every instance when Williams had a good idea, because it was so rare. But he did have a point. Assuming that he and JB hadn't gone too overboard in fungus consumption, there was a decent chance that we had enough mushrooms to jack up every trailer park in Kentucky.

"Guys, we've gotta start working on that short-term memory thing," Jimmy threw in. "Does anyone remember Williams pontificating on the evolution of the black race? I'm gonna go ahead and file for a mushroom exemption on his ass. No mushrooms for Williams."

Williams and Jimmy stared at each other for a few minutes.

It was pretty comical on the surface. And really, Williams was the only one who risked an ass beating.

So, while staring at Jim, Williams reached into the supply box. He pulled out one of the two large bags of shrooms. He then slowly and meticulously pulled out a big-ass mushroom and placed it on his extended tongue. He rolled his tongue inward around it and began to chew. He then followed his aggressive swallow with an ear-to-ear grin.

Jimmy just stared.

"You know I will not hesitate to grind your cracker ass into dust if you start up again, right?" he said at last.

"Always a race thing," said Williams, shaking his head. "Jesus, Jim, I thought we covered that long ago. Live in the now, bro. I'll see you on the other side."

At that point, we all wondered whether Williams would live through the night. Only time would tell.

Into the wild psychedelic yonder yet again we delved. About a half hour or so after we chowed down on the mushrooms, my hair began to tingle. Everyone in the crew was beginning to feel the effects.

I had initially decided that it would be best if I was the one who held on to the flare gun. Just to be safe. But when I noticed that I was gripping it tightly with both hands, like a cop in pursuit of a perp, I questioned that decision.

The walls of the canyon, which earlier had seemed to rise straight upward from the water, now seemed to be bending over us. They would bend inward and then go back . . . bend and then go back . . . almost as if the canyon was chewing us.

It was times like this that you could really *feel* life.

The awareness of any sort of line between the conscious and subconscious was blurred. The great philosophical propellers on our boats began to turn, and we could not shy away from them.

"So," I said. "My brain has gone apeshit on me. Before I lose it, could someone throw me a beer?"

JB opened the ice chest. It seemed like it was nine feet away from him, due to a mushroom-induced ape-arm illusion, yet he easily reached inside. He swirled his hand around the ice for a moment, then put his other hand inside and swirled it around, too.

"Dude," I repeated. "Beer."

"Shit," he replied. "Sorry. But you should see this. There's an entire world in here."

Eventually, he tossed me a beer. It was overthrown and not really anywhere in my general direction at all. It sailed overhead, leaving a glimmering silver tracer arc in its wake before finally splashing down fantastically in the river. We were all transfixed by its glory. Even though none of us would ever drink that beer, we all enjoyed it.

"This is how life should be," I said. "Sure, I guess in a perfect world, I'd be able to drink a beer while watching a beer be thrown, but that was going to be my beer, because I don't have a beer, but still . . . This is great. Fucking Jorge doesn't know shit."

"You guys remember that story by Plato about the cave?" Jimmy asked.

"I remember JB's mom having a vagina like a cave," Devero said, "but I don't remember if Plato ever wrote about it. He probably tapped that ass, though. Don't get me wrong."

He chuckled, then he took a mossball to the face.

"Plato had this parable," Jimmy continued. "It's called the Allegory of the Cave . . . I think. I'm seeing shit everywhere. But that's probably what it was called.

"So, this guy gains consciousness in a cave," he went on, "and he has no memory of anything. He's chained facing the wall. There's a fire behind him, illuminating the cave. In between him and the fire are puppets. The puppets are casting shadows on the wall he's facing. The guy can't see behind him, so the only light source he knows about is the reflection of light on the wall. The only other creatures he knows about are the shadows of puppets on the wall. He assumes that this is the way life is.

"But then, one day, he's turned around and he's chained up *facing* the fire. He sees the fire. He sees the puppets. He discovers that *this* is actually the way life is, not the way he'd known before. Light is not a reflection; it's a fire. The shadows aren't other beings; the puppets are the other beings. He accepts this as what is real.

"Then, all of the shit in his world gets shaken up again. He gets freed from his chains. He leaves the cave altogether, where he sees the real sun and real people. And again, he realizes he was wrong about what reality was. I don't know why I just thought of that, but it seems pretty applicable."

"Shit, what the hell is that supposed to mean?" JB inquired.

"It means," Jim said, "that we always think we have the answer. But one little shift by God can show us we don't know shit."

"Or maybe God is one of those things we've got to realize isn't real," I said. "For thousands of years, anything we've been unable to comprehend or explain has been automatically ascribed to God. But then science figures it out, and it isn't God at all. We get turned away from the wall of the cave every day, man, but people want to keep staring at the wall. Don't you ever feel like we've evolved enough as a civilization to leave the whole 'God did it' thing behind?"

"It's about faith, man," Jimmy replied.

"Yeah, Jimmy, but what if faith is just the chain keeping you facing the wall?" I said.

"To me, the evidence is all around us that God is here," he answered. "Look at this canyon, the beauty of it. How could this not be the work of God?"

"Well, Jim," Williams said, jumping in. "This canyon can easily be explained. Not to deny God, mind you, but this canyon *has been* explained by science. A geologist would tell you that the Rio Grande formed this canyon over millions of years. According to God, this planet wasn't even here millions of years ago."

"Jesus, guys," Devero shot out, staring at me. "I get so tired of everyone looking down their nose at people just for believing in God. You guys just can't admit that there have been some *seriously* intelligent people who believed in God. You ride this intellectual high horse of atheism or agnosticism. Isn't there something to be said for actually *believing* in something? You talk about God like he's the fucking Easter Bunny. It's so goddamned condescending."

"I've gotta piss," groused Williams. "Someone should condescend to roll me a joint."

Williams stood up to pee. He went to put his leg up on the edge of the boat for balance, but he completely missed. He fell forward, grabbing at the air for anything to save him, and found nothing.

Boom. Right in the water. Again.

Williams didn't help matters by being entirely unable to pull his fat ass up into the boat. He must have fallen back in the water five times. Each time, we laughed harder. By the time he finally made it into the boat, I thought I would need surgery to repair serious internal damage from convulsive laughter.

I've thought it many times but became certain of this only then: There is nothing in existence that is funnier than someone falling down. Seeing an animal fall down is a very close second, because we don't expect animals to lose their balance. Old people farting is right up there on the list also, because you don't know if they just couldn't hear how loud the fart was or if they did it just to say, *Fuck you, world. I've earned the right to fart whenever I damn well please.* But people falling down is some seriously funny shit. It still ranks number one.

A short time later, we saw a little chunk of land protruding out into the river. It would be just big enough for all of our sleeping bags and a campfire.

These little protruding land chunks were rare. The cliffs shot vertically from the water for nearly every inch of the canyon's length. We had to take advantage of this one, since we didn't know when another one would come along.

We agreed that this would be an excellent piece of real estate upon which to temporarily halt our rafting trip while we pursued our mushroom trip.

There was hardly enough space to park both boats on this tiny land chunk, so we tied the boats together and tied the first one to the branch of a small tree. We unloaded our gear, chuckling at anything and everything. We had moved from mellowness to exhaustion to giddiness.

The night crept up on us and caught us unawares. The stars were on full display. The sky looked like a living Picasso.

As I stood on the riverbank, staring upward at what looked like a hallway to Heaven between the canyon walls, I had to think to myself that perhaps Jim had a point. I knew that science could explain what I saw, but maybe only a god could make it that magnificent. Maybe. Or maybe that was the mushrooms. That whole Big Bang thing might have made a little more sense.

We needed to make a campfire. Normally, only one of us would have made the fire, but this time it was a group effort. And because we had continued to eat the psychedelic shroomies, the fire had a particularly alluring quality to it. It would grow large and then shrink again. Maybe I was the only one who saw it. That didn't appear to be the case, though. When it went small again, I did what I thought any sensible outdoorsman would do. I shot it with the flare gun.

It was immediately recognized as a bad idea. We were all blinded for a couple of minutes. I wish I could tell you that everyone took it well. Following the glorious light show, which was missing only a Pink Floyd soundtrack, I became the second person to be banned from the flare gun.

Everyone then shifted their attention from the fire to the ground beef. It was time to make patties. We were like a group of kindergartners playing with Play-Doh. Before taking the shape of hamburger patties, each of our individual meat clumps had taken on many forms. Mine had been both a fighter plane and an elephant. Devero made a giraffe, while JB made a finely crafted Bob Marley head, complete with dreadlocks. Jim made a crucifix, which I believe he briefly prayed to. Williams made a large penis.

"I bet you can't wait to dig into that," Jimmy said.

Then we deconstructed our art, threw it on the fire, and began to chow down.

Moments after the burgers had vanished, I noticed us all staring at the cliff.

The cliff was taunting us. Climbing a cliff that was at least two hundred feet high would be a challenge in the dark. Then we had to factor in the mushrooms, whiskey, beer, and weed.

"We're gonna have to climb it," JB said. "We have no choice."

"We're gonna need a big joint for this one," Devero replied.

34

I can't begin to tell you how cool the climb was. Most people would have been overcome with fear about twenty feet up, like Williams was—but even Williams kept climbing.

He began to cry about halfway up, but he kept climbing.

Every ten feet or so, I would turn and look around. The higher I got, the bigger the sky became. I could almost reach out and grab the constellations.

It was like "Jack and the Beanstalk," only at night and with a jagged, painful beanstalk and hallucinogens.

It's very easy to put aside the pain in your muscles and skin when you know that dropping to your death is the only alternative to hanging on. But it was a difficult climb. Thankfully, as we neared the top, a section of the lip on the cliff edged back like a staircase.

Devero was the first to reach the summit, followed closely by Jimmy and me. Then came JB, who had gone slowly to coach

Williams and provide moral support for him. Once we had reached the top, we all moved a few feet downriver to a section that hung outward over the water. There was a collective collapsing of our youthful bodies. We lay back with our feet dangling over the edge.

"Hey, Williams," Jimmy said.

"Yo."

"Did I hear you crying?"

"I was grunting. I wasn't crying."

"You're a pussy."

"Screw you, Afro Man."

"Pussy. Crybaby pussy."

"Well, I was grunting because of this," Williams yelled angrily, pulling a half gallon of Knob Creek whiskey out of his backpack. "It was grinding into my back the whole way up. I was gonna just drop it after a while, but this is some expensive shit."

"Holy shit, man," Jimmy said, beaming with pride. "I apologize. I thought you were just being your usual little self—you know, a pussy. I had no idea you were taking one for the team. Nicely done."

Williams worked at the lid of the bottle as another stare-down ensued. The bottle of whiskey washed away my fear that the weight of Jim and Williams on this overhang would force us to live out a Wile E. Coyote moment, with this section breaking off.

We passed the bottle down the line in one direction, and we passed a joint in the other. I guess we were saving the question of "How in the holy shit do we get back down?" for later.

Forever had passed without a spoken word. The joint finally died, and over half the bottle of whiskey was gone. We were all just taking it in and enjoying the silence. It seemed like we all understood how rare and great the quiet was. We all wanted it to last a while.

Well . . . all of us but Williams.

"Guys, I've been an asshole on this trip," he blurted out suddenly.

"You've been an asshole ever since I've known you," JB replied.

"Thanks. But seriously. I've been a prick. I'm sorry."

The apology lingered for a bit. No one replied, most likely because of how squarely he had hit the nail on the head.

I sat up and looked down at the water. You couldn't see the boats or our campsite because of the way the cliff bent back. You could just see the reflection of the fire far down below.

I was starting to think that we would have to spend the night up there. We had taken *shitfaced* to a new level.

Williams was the kind of guy who could only go one of two directions when he got this hammered: He became an emotional basket case or an extreme asshole. Thankfully, the emotional basket case was the Williams we had gotten this night. We would have thrown the asshole over the edge.

"Here's the thing, guys," he said. "I lied: I don't have a job waiting for me anymore."

He paused for a moment, trying to add dramatic effect. It was probably intentional, but you couldn't tell, because he was seldom sincere. And you never really know who's fucking with you when you're on shrooms.

"My mom called me a few days ago," he continued. "Apparently, not only has my dad been paying off some lady he'd been screwing to keep her quiet, but he also fucked over some investors on some big deal."

Now he was actually crying. Great. Maybe I should have wished for his asshole alter ego after all. We didn't need this shit right now.

"The family business is finished—done," Williams sobbed. "We're gonna lose everything. He tied all of our personal shit to this deal to make it happen, and now it's all gonna fold. My car, my job, my future . . ." He started to cry uncontrollably.

I put my arm around him. It felt a little fake, because I couldn't help thinking about how badly he was killing the buzz. *What a dick.* But I guess he couldn't help it this time. We were the only people in the world he could talk to.

"Are you kidding me?" Devero asked. "How could that possibly happen? Your dad has a shitload of money. He's got a huge-ass mansion in Colorado. He's got a huge-ass boat. He's got a fucking airplane. How could he lose it all?"

"I guess it's been going on for a while," Williams cried. "Shit started going south, and he attached everything to some deal to keep it going. Then it all started happening too fast to outrun.

"He inflated the value on the deal to some investors and used the money from them to pay off that chick. This chick is, like, twenty-five, man. And she's fat, too. God dammit! He doesn't give a shit about me. He just pissed my future away for money and a fat piece of ass."

He was bawling and managing to be near blacklisted from future trips.

"That's hardcore," Jimmy said. "But it's not the end of the world. You're a sharp guy, man. You'll land on your feet. You know any of us will make calls for you. You'll be fine. We can't do shit about how fat and bald you are, though."

"Thanks, Jim. Dammit, I've been such a dick to you. I'm sorry, man. There's no excuse for it."

"Yeah, I guess I can't exactly whip out pictures of JB holding his dick next to your mouth or you wearing a black man's ass as a hat at a time like this," Jimmy said.

"Where the fuck did that come from?" Williams exclaimed. "I'm trying to be serious right now. I'm really emotional."

I made the *not right now* throat-cutting motion to Jimmy with my hand as we all looked away to keep from laughing.

"Sorry, bro," Jimmy said with a poker face that made it even harder for us not to laugh. "We're here for you."

Williams kept crying, and Jimmy kept trying to comfort him. I guess you couldn't blame Williams for being so inconsolable; the guy had been set to make a quarter million a year pretty soon after college. And what else did he have? No matter what Jimmy said, Williams wasn't all that sharp. He would be lucky to get twenty grand a year with his social skills. He'd never had a boss in his life that he hadn't been able to tell to kiss his ass. That kind of job security was gone now. I guess we were all he had left. And that sucked, because we all liked him so much less now.

"Jim, man, I didn't mean that shit I was saying," Williams sobbed. "That's not me. It's just not. I can't believe the shit I said to you. Especially after your brother . . . your dad . . . my god, how can you still even look at me?"

"Unless I kill you and sink your ass in the river, I don't really have a choice," Jimmy said. "But I'm all about forgiveness, man. That's what my man JC would want."

"I've read the Bible, Jimmy," I said. "Jesus never punched anybody out or used his ass as a hat."

"I'm working on that," Jimmy replied as Williams again gave us a look of bewilderment. "Jesus is all that's got me through this last year . . . Jesus and you guys. Williams, you've just gotta have faith that you can get through all of this.

"I hope you really don't mean all of that shit you said. It was bad. That shit will corrode your soul. That's what evil sounds like. That's what the guy who killed my dad and brother sounded like. And your dad may be terrible, but at least you're still gonna have a dad. You should come to church with me."

"Yeah, I wouldn't stick out there," Williams snorted.

"Nobody cares there, man. You should go."

"That's lame," I said. "You shouldn't teach people to use religion as a crutch. Then they won't develop any sensible way of dealing with things. It doesn't seem right."

"Why can't you just let go of your anger against God, Legs?" Jimmy asked me. "Why are you so against religion now? You seem so cynical."

"I just like to make educated decisions about the really big shit," I returned. "I don't think Jesus will get the stockholders of Williams Enterprises together and undo all the fraud. Jesus won't get Williams's dad to unfuck the fatty. And I don't think that believing in Jesus just because your parents do is making an educated decision."

"Neither is being a Republican just because your dad is," he said back.

"Wow," I replied. "Touché. You've got a point. It's all about geography, man. It's all about where you're born."

"I'll make you a deal," Jimmy said. "I'll become a Republican if you'll believe in God."

"I guess you wouldn't stick out any more in the Republican Party than Williams would at your church."

Williams laughed a little, wiping away his tears. We all felt bad for the guy. And there was no question he was going to feel like an ass tomorrow when we made fun of him for crying tonight.

One by one, we began passing out. We had moved a good distance from the edge of the cliff so that no one would die from simply rolling over in their sleep.

Jimmy and I were the last ones awake. We stole Williams's pack of smokes and headed back to the cliff. We sat down a good distance from where we had been earlier. There was a straight drop down to the river here. We smoked our cigarettes with our feet dangling over the drop.

"This is amazing," I said.

And it was. There wasn't a cloud in the sky. Stars shot across the sky every few seconds. They were so bright and so clear. And the moon was huge. It was like the gigantic, mesmerizing eye of some strange celestial voyeur, watching us in amazement as we stared back.

"You don't think God painted that picture for you?" Jimmy asked.

"I can't honestly say one way or the other, Jimmy," I answered. "But how do you know you got the right one, man? How do you know you got it right? If you got it wrong, it's damnation and eternal pits of fire."

"There you go again. You've got to get this fundamentalist stereotype out of your head. You've got to learn what a parable is. Not all of us want our chicks in veils and robes. I don't think anybody can say who is and isn't going to Hell. Maybe God visited different people at different times. Maybe he sent more than one messenger of his word. I don't know; it's not my place. But seeing a sight like this humbles me. I realize that I can't begin to understand God."

"I've never met a Christian before who didn't try to speak for God," I said softly but with conviction. "They have no problem condemning anyone who doesn't believe exactly as they do. Christians today have nothing in common with Jesus. Do you think they help poor people? Do you think they don't judge? You hit it on the head when you mentioned parables; they don't have a clue what a parable is. They pick and choose whichever passages support them being assholes and justify it under the banner of God. It makes me sick. They are hijacking morality and turning it on its head."

"Did you say *help poor people?*" Jimmy said, laughing. "Now you sound like a Democrat. I guess I may not save your soul, but I might get your vote."

"Ha. Don't count on either. I don't think my soul needs saving. That's like when people say they're going to pray for me. It's nice and all, but why would the god they believe in want to help me?"

"All you've gotta do is ask, man. He'll help."

I always respected and admired Jimmy for his unquenchable desire to help others and save their souls. But when we got into the deep stuff in our debates, I didn't think it had a place. I didn't think *just ask him* and *have faith* were tools to argue with. It got under my skin a little.

"Stop trying to save me, Jim. It ain't happening; I don't need it. Besides, I walked down the aisle to be saved, like, eight times growing up. Every year at summer camp, I would go get me some Jesus. No one ever told me I just had to go once. They let it go on for years.

"But did it do anything for me?" I asked mockingly. "Did it make me big and strong? Hell no. I prayed to not be such a stringy little bastard, but it didn't work. I kept getting screwed. Did Jesus keep me away from drugs? Did he help me get good grades? Did he help me follow my dreams? Not at all."

"Drugs and grades?" Jimmy questioned with amazement. "Following your dreams? Have you ever heard of personal accountability? Don't you think you had more to do with that shit than God? You think God's got something against you? Look around the world, man. Look around the country. You think you got it bad? Really? How many people you think would trade places with how bad you got it? You ain't a realist, man; you're just bitter because you know you're smarter than a lot of people but you ain't done shit about it. And you look at the masses in that condescending way— just blaming, blaming your unhappiness on them. You're gonna have to reconcile with yourself someday."

"You don't understand what it's like to be as small as I am—just physically *weak* in comparison to everybody else. I've gone through life knowing that if I stand up to anyone, I risk a humiliating ass beating. But if I don't stand up, I get humiliated anyway. And those jock bastards know it. They know who to pick on.

"It just rips your dignity away, man," I fumed. "And those fuckers look for the right setting. The bigger the audience, the bigger the laugh. Or when I'm talking to a chick . . . My whole life, you know? Who wants to date the guy who can't stand up for himself? People look at me and think I'm so skinny that I look *sick*, man! You just said it yourself!"

I sat quietly, reliving the humiliation I'd been subject to my entire life as I stared off into the distance. I tried to focus on the beauty of the sky to calm down, but I couldn't walk away from a good debate. Especially this one.

"I've always tried to be a good person, Jim. I prayed to God so many nights for years and years to just make me look *normal*. And he never answered, man. He left me here to get beat up and laughed at and didn't do shit. Surely, if this god is so just, so magnificent, so full of love, he might answer just *one simple prayer*. But no! Never! So if that love's not real, then maybe he's not real. Maybe God is just another fairy tale to calm the herds."

"Maybe it's about more than our selfish needs. Maybe it's more about a plan that he has for us."

"Really? And what did God do for you? Did he keep your dad and brother out of harm's way? Has God ever let anything good happen to you? Is that part of the plan? Shit, Jim, I just don't see the logic. You of all people."

"You just can't look at it like that," Jimmy said gently, pushing back. "In those months after half my family was ripped away by that sick fuck—when I was in my bedroom at night and I could hear my mom crying in the other room—I *cursed* God, man. I *cursed* him. I couldn't understand why he did this.

"My brother . . . he was just such a sweet, innocent kid. And my dad was a good man. He had flaws, you know, but I just kept thinking that God didn't really care about me. I was getting some pretty good signs pointing that way.

"But something changed," he said as he turned to look at me. "I knew I had a choice. We've all got a choice. *We* decide how happy we want to be. You can either trust God or curse him; I just decided to trust him. I can't explain it, but it helped me, and I can't deny that."

I sighed, shaking my head.

"Well . . . I don't think I curse God," I said. "I just don't claim to know whether he exists or not. I can't claim that if there is a god that I could ever begin to understand him. I think that would be arrogant. And once you've entered this mindset, I don't think it's possible to go back.

"It's like when you find out Santa Claus isn't real. You can never go back to believing in him. I wish I could. I wish I knew that I would see my closest friends and family in some afterlife, but it just doesn't make sense. I can't make it back to that place."

"Well, I'll pray for you."

"Kiss my ass."

Jimmy and me having these talks now and then was therapy for both of us. I think the contrarian nature of my friendship somehow strengthened his faith. I knew his faith was genuine, not that hypocritical "Send us your money" evangelical bullshit. Maybe his constant nagging was the only thing that made me think that it was remotely possible that there could be a god, and maybe I wanted to keep that hope alive.

Or maybe the mushrooms and weed had a symbiotic relationship with the spiritual, and I had locked myself into that world yet remained devoid of it.

I looked over at Jim. He was sitting up. His eyes were closing. He was swaying a bit back and forth. It suddenly dawned on me that we were sitting on the edge of a cliff.

Then, it started to happen, as if in slow motion. Jim's head fell forward, and his torso followed after.

I screamed his name and dove toward him, catching his shirt by the neck.

Just as gravity almost owned him, I managed a brief moment of leverage. With the collar of his shirt clutched firmly in my hand, I swung his body backward with all my might.

His head slammed back on the ground behind him, finally waking him up with an alarming jolt.

"What the fuck? Oh, Jesus! What happened?" Jimmy screamed, dazed.

"You passed out on the edge of a cliff, dumbass!"

"My fucking head hurts, man. Was that shit necessary?"

"I guess we could have picked you up in the morning."

And with that, we headed back to the spot where everyone else was scattered. They were all just lying carelessly on the rough ground, snoozing away on sticks and rocks.

I thought that there would be no possible way I would ever go to sleep, as I positioned my T-shirt under the back of my head, giving me thin insulation from the jagged ground.

And then I drifted off.

Getting back down was much easier than we thought it would be. Devero had brought up two hundred and fifty feet of climbing rope and five harnesses in his backpack.

I have no clue how he remembered to bring the gear, but it sure made life better.

We tied the rope to a tree and rappelled over the edge one at a time. JB and I went face-first, while the other guys did the whole backward-jumping thing.

Jimmy was the only one who didn't throw up on the way down. Because of the vomit everywhere, we decided to eat our granola bars on the boats and stuck them in our pockets as we elected our newest Q-boat captain.

Rock, paper, scissors . . . Jim was stuck on the Q boat. Although it had no doubt benefited him multiple times thus far in his life, the size of his penis couldn't get him out of this one.

"I'll see if I can say this without throwing up again," I said. "Jorge, that little rat bastard, might have said something about rapids today. Maybe. God, I would kick his ass right now. Anyhow, we should be careful."

"You say that every day," Jimmy said. "Devero, for the love of all that is holy, please roll us a joint to take the pain away."

"It's gonna cost you a beer," he replied.

"How could you drink a beer right now?" Jimmy asked and then paused. "Actually, damn . . . I hate to say it, but that sounds pretty fucking good right now. Anyone else?"

We were all takers. My god, did that beer taste good.

My grandfather, who was a great guy, had a tendency to drink way too much. I remembered fishing with him when I was growing up. Just before the sun would come up, we would leave the double-wide trailer he lived in with my grandmother at Lake Granbury, walk out the back door to his pontoon boat, and head across the lake to his favorite fishing spot. We would tie the boat up to a section of trees that were peeking their heads above the water, near a point on the east side of the lake, and we would catch the sun rising gloriously. I remembered that, in the morning, Grandpa (I called him Freddy) would crack open a can of Coors Original and pour a little salt on the lid. I could always tell that the first beer was his favorite. And now I understood why.

With the beer in us, our hangovers came to a screeching halt. Our headaches and upset stomachs were postponed by our good friends beer and weed. Over the next hour or so, instead of getting sick, we got wasted again. We finished off the bottle of whiskey we had opened the night before.

Thankfully, we had known how much beer we would be drinking on this trip and erred on the side of caution when packing the essentials. But we still felt the need to protect the beer—to conserve it by introducing liquor from time to time. Sometimes we would even sip an occasional splash of water. Healthy living.

The hunger pains began to hit us around lunchtime. Go figure. There were no caves to duck into this time, though. There were no patches of land to pull our boats onto, either. So we became a floating cafeteria.

Our sandwiches were thrown together in a most haphazard fashion. Our Doritos got soggy from our beer-drenched hands. The beer and Doritos combined to make the bread of our sandwiches orange while offering the hidden benefit of increased flavor.

Oh, also, we stank. Bad.

We came to a turn in the canyon, and the water picked up slightly. The turn was timed impeccably with the sun blasting over the wall. The canyon lit up all at once, again grabbing our yearning souls and thrusting us back to life. Without hesitation, like a synchronized team, we cast ourselves over the sides of the boats yet again.

Devero remained aboard, working like mad to get a joint together for the occasion. When the task was completed, he tossed everyone their life vests and an ice-cold beer, lit the joint, and gently lowered himself into the water.

He was a careful man—a man with a plan.

We positioned our life vests underneath our asses to serve as seats. A circle of compadres was formed, and the joint began its rotation.

If someday I were to become Secretary General of the United Nations, the heads of all major countries on this globe would be required to join me in a conference of ass jackets, joints, and cold beer. Only then would we make progress.

Even when the life of the doob had passed, our circle stayed connected. Williams went back for more beers as the sun left us yet again. He tossed the frosties around and grabbed the rope that was tied to the front of the boat. He tied the free end of the rope to his life vest, put the vest on, and cannonballed into the river. He was determined to not be forced into chasing the boats again.

Unfortunately for Williams, being tied to the boat caused him to be nominated to fetch about twenty more rounds of beer. At least. The first couple of times, he bitchingly obliged by making individual trips back up into the boat for us. It bothered him to do things for others. After that, we would just wait until he finished his beer and have him pitch us ours when he went to get one for himself. We knew he couldn't make it long without beer, and he knew we knew that. His back was against the wall.

He passed out at one point with a doobie in his mouth. The doobie then fell from his lips onto the front of his rented life vest, where it burned a big-ass hole. I think we were all secretly hoping he'd burst into flames, but he didn't. He woke up just as the life vest began to let off a huge puff of toxic smoke. We laughed our asses off.

"Goddammit! You fuckers! I could've caught on fire!" he screamed, after he'd doused the flames. "I could've died from smoke inhalation!"

"I know, man, that's why we didn't say anything," Jimmy said, chuckling.

"Great," Williams went on griping. "Now I have to pay for a fucking rented life vest. I'm just gonna stash it in my backpack at the end and hope Jorge keeps his fucking mouth shut."

Damn. We were so close to being rid of him.

The next time he went to get himself a beer, he looked over at us. We were all looking right back at him. He knew he was our bitch today, and it didn't sit well with him.

"What do you fuckers want now, huh? Another round of beers?" he yelled at us. "Can I mix anyone a goddamn martini this time?"

"Listen, bro," JB hollered back, "you're the genius who tied himself to the boat. And you have to know that most reasonable folks would have killed you two days ago. So the only way we can let that slide is if you get beers for us. So stop crying and toss me a beer, dingleberry."

"Yeah, douchebag," Devero shouted, "have you heard me bitch about rolling nine thousand joints on this trip?"

"Jesus, you turd," I jumped in. "Not to mention, Devero is risking it *all* just being here with us because his mom humped some Saudi dude twenty-something years ago behind his dad's back. We're all sacrificing, man."

"Hey, speaking of joints," Jimmy added, "why don't you put your bald, fat, crying ass to the task of throwing one of those together too?"

"One step ahead of you, my dark-skinned brother," Devero said. "Williams, move your chunky ass over to my backpack; I prerolled a few. One less thing for you to bitch about. There's a lighter in one of the other pockets. If you won't cry about it around the fire tonight, maybe you could grab that shit for us."

"Are you guys done?" Williams asked as he rummaged through the backpack. "Thanks for all the confidence building. I love it when people draw attention to the effects of my slow metabolism. I also love it when . . . What the fuck? When did . . . Holy shit! You motherfuckers!"

Williams sat down slowly as he lifted a stack of Polaroids from the backpack. He stared painstakingly at each and every one of them.

"Oh, damn," I said. "Wrong backpack, dude. Just put those back and grab a doobie."

"Holy shit, man!" Williams screamed. "How in the *hell* could you guys ever call *me* twisted?"

"Dude," Devero said, "the weed is in the blue backpack. Seriously, man. We feel the need—the need for weed!"

"Jimmy, I reached out to you, man!" Williams said in

bewilderment. "And you let your asshole kiss my head! And whose friggin' pecker is that, huh? Oh, wait, tighty-whities . . . JB, you have problems, man."

"Yeah, we all do," JB replied. "At least I didn't put it in your mouth. Well, not all the way. Just grab a joint, dude. You can visit your therapist when you get back."

"I might as well tell you right now, man: I farted on your head," Jimmy stated plainly. "Bare ass on a bald head, man, it was like, *pow!*"

"Oh, so you know," I added, "Jim's fart sounded pretty wet. If you get a chance, you should dip your head in the water a few times . . . maybe rub it with a napkin."

"You might even use toilet paper, amigo," JB threw in. "And hey, you know I love you, whether you have shit marks on your head or not."

"And you do," Devero said flatly. "You do have shit marks on your head."

We were on a roll.

Williams stared us all down and stuffed all of the pictures, one by one, into the empty bottle of Knob Creek whiskey. He then poured lighter fluid into the bottle and dropped a match inside.

"Sorry to spoil your fun, homos, but these won't be making the trip home with us," he said with pride as he held up the bottle.

Unfortunately for Williams, the glass got extremely hot extremely quickly. He let out a scream, and as he turned to throw the bottle in the river, his footing gave way again.

He fell forward and hit his head on the inflatable side of the boat so hard that it damn near bounced him back upright. Then his other foot slipped, and for the nine hundred thousandth time, he fell into the water. He was like having a regular fucking Benny Hill on the boat, with the exception of the asshole white-supremacy thing.

We watched in amazement as the accidentally thrown bottle left a trail of liquid fire while sailing a good fifty yards away, before slowly sinking, like a ship lost in battle.

Williams reemerged from the water a short time later, looking pissed. But he always looked pissed.

He probably just needed to be punched again.

37

The sun soon passed out of the canyon again. It didn't bother us a bit. The size of our circle was in direct correlation to our degree of alcoholic intake. Beers being tossed by Williams were missed by ever-widening margins, possibly due to his utter humiliation.

While we could have kept talking for days about Williams being caught spanking it or the pictures taken in the aftermath, we slowly and mercifully let it die.

After a while, Williams's attitude dipped back to its normal asshole level.

Then the temptation of giving in to serenity again won our bodies over. The circle, which once was connected, somewhat naturally dispersed, and we began to drift farther and farther apart.

The now-familiar heightened state of relaxation robbed us of our attention. Only in the powers of levitation could this feeling of weightlessness have been beaten. We floated late into the afternoon. The shadows continued to make strides in their battle with daylight.

As our minds were doing the tango on the dance floor of the netherworld, a sensation slowly stirred my thoughts. Had the water begun to pick up speed? That seemingly constant noise . . . had it gotten louder?

I jumped so fast that I nearly came out of the water.

Everyone was scattered at wide distances, napping on their life vests just as they had the day before. Williams, still tied to the boat and now unconscious, had been pulled a good bit ahead of us. He was about to go over, from my estimation, a significant drop.

I screamed for everyone to wake up, scanning the canyon walls frantically for some safe haven where we could dock. There was nothing.

Williams jolted awake and turned to look around just as the boat to which he was tied disappeared over the falls. The terrified look on all of our faces reflected the concern that Williams might not have had time to get his feet in front of him.

Feet first! Feet first! Feet first! It had been beaten into our heads for years, from the first time we ever stepped into a raft on a river.

The rope was tied to Williams's back. It was pulling him hard and may have made "feet first" entirely impossible for him.

And only at the edge could we really see what lay ahead of us: an insanely wild row of rapids, huge waves crashing upon massive boulders, tremendous drops. The violence of it literally took my breath away, consuming me with a fear like nothing I'd ever known. This was what death looked like. The aquatic madness went on as far as I could see in that brief second before I went over.

One by one, we were each sucked over the edge.

I only had time to get my life jacket over my right shoulder. I was spun and whipped so wildly and madly that I felt lucky to have the vest at all. The first set of falls threw me onto rocks that crushed all of the breath out of my lungs. No matter how hard I gasped, I couldn't get enough air. I landed hard on my left arm after at least a twenty-foot drop. I knew I had scraped a sizeable section of skin off and probably broken some ribs.

The pain and speed of everything—the inability to breathe, the inability to even know which way was up . . . it paralyzed my body. I couldn't even fight. I still couldn't move my damaged arm enough to get my vest on, and I continued to struggle to keep my other arm secure.

Screams and flashes of other life vests were the only evidence that the others were still alive and nearby.

Another huge drop. Madness. Levels of pain that I never knew existed. The roar of the falls nearly drowned out the screams of my friends. Their minds and bodies had been overtaken by terror, just as mine had been.

I was suddenly flipped upside-down and smashed my forehead on the razor-sharp edge of a rock. I was blinded by blood and the throbbing of the blow to my head as I was hurled upright again. Tears and blood streamed down my face as I screamed.

I somehow got my feet in front of me and gained some sense of direction, and I managed an almost imperceptible level of control.

Then, yet another huge drop.

I braced myself for the harsh impact I'd felt over the last several drops. I thought I'd been shown a bit of grace when I didn't slam into anything upon reaching the bottom of the fall, but this was torture in disguise. This time, as I plunged deep beneath the surface, the hands of death grabbed me and wouldn't let go. The current of the undertow seemed to pull harder and harder downward the more I fought.

I struggled for air, literally dying to reach the surface—fighting, flailing my arms, kicking my legs. It hurt my head so much to go that long without being able to take a breath. I was just about ready to give in when I remembered "Go with it."

"Go with it" was what we'd been trained to do when this very thing happened. It wasn't the undercurrent that generally killed people; it was the fight. I had to go limp and let it take me.

I quit fighting. I really had no energy left to fight, anyhow. The current had me in some sort of death roll—but, as I went limp, it slowly released me and pushed me to the surface.

I sucked in as much air as possible in my first gasp, preparing for the unknown. I had a moment to look around and try to gather my thoughts. Ahead, I could see that the Q boat had flipped and dumped all our inventory. Williams had pulled himself onto the edge of the other boat, which was whipping and twisting wildly over the falls. I couldn't see any of the others. I had to assume that they were thrashing madly somewhere behind me.

I thought I heard Devero and JB yelling to each other somewhere at a distance, but the acoustics of the canyon could play tricks on you. You often couldn't tell where a sound came from.

Williams grabbed an oar to try to slow his boat. He had no control. He was screaming, searching erratically for the others while trying to stop the boat from spinning. He came around to face me every few seconds. He was about a hundred yards ahead, but I knew that he could see me, because our eyes met each time. I was desperately clinging to life in hopes that he might somehow be able to help.

Then, for a brief moment, we both stole a glance at something that had just gone over the falls between us. Over the next drop, we saw it again. It was Jim.

I screamed at the top of my lungs. Williams did the same.

Jim threw an arm up in agony as he was battered by the rocks, and for a very brief moment, the roaring waves subsided—but not for long.

We looked downriver in terror, seeing that we weren't anywhere near done with this.

The guys behind me were crying out more loudly than any of us, adding an additional element of chaotic salt to this wound.

Jimmy struggled to pull himself closer to Williams, who had begun casting out the thirty-foot rope that had been tied to his jacket. The current, as well as Williams's inability to balance himself in a spinning boat, were keeping any level of accuracy at bay.

There was a gruesome gash in the back of Jimmy's head. You could make out a red tinge in the water downriver from him. He had lost his vest and was struggling with one mangled arm to keep his head above the surface. He was fighting hard, but the river appeared to be winning.

I was trying with all of my being to get to him.

He and Williams were yelling to one another. I could barely make out what they were saying over the crashing of the waves.

"Throw me your jacket!" Jimmy cried.

"I can't! Just get closer!" Williams yelled back. He was crying also, overwhelmed.

"Throw it to me! I can't stay up, man! I'm hurt bad!"

"Just come closer to me! I'll get you!"

"Throw him your fucking jacket, man! He's fucking dying!" I screamed at Williams from a distance, now able to comprehend what was happening.

"I can't, man. I fucking can't! I'll fucking die!"

"You're in the boat!" I yelled, "Throw him your fucking jacket!"

"Williams," Jim pleaded, "please, God, please help me! I can't stay up! God, please help me!"

The calm amid the chaos disappeared as Williams again vanished over another fall. I had closed the distance between Jim and myself considerably, but it wasn't enough. I followed just a few feet behind him over the next fall.

At that moment, my mind snapped a picture that I'm certain can never be erased. Jim went over backward, headfirst. We never lost eye contact from the moment we went over to the moment his head collided with a jagged boulder the size of a car. The crooked edge of the rock kept his head in place for just a second, while the torrents of the water turned his body to the feet-first position. And fate timed it so that we dropped from there side by side, eyes locked. I caught a flash of blood and tissue stuck to the boulder that stole my best friend from me, just as it let go of him. I finally made it to him, grabbed his sleeve, and commanded my weary hand to not let it go.

This wasn't happening. This couldn't be happening. As I wept and screamed at the limp body next to me, my mind wouldn't let me accept what I'd seen.

I couldn't feel the pain of the rocks smashing my own body to bits after that. I held on to him, rolling over fall after fall, trying without success to get his head above water. Even though the back of his head was soft, shattered, and torn open, I tried to keep it above water. As the water gradually slowed, I could finally pull my body up behind Jim, with my arm under his chin to keep his nose and mouth above water.

My own disbelief masked the wails from the others. They were banged up badly, but they could all see that Jimmy was much worse. They could tell he hadn't made it.

I couldn't hear the crying at all. I just stared into the abyss. And it was staring right back at me now—glaring, judging, laughing with some sick scowl of righteous indignation.

A rope landed beside me, jolting me back into reality. JB and Devero were in the water right in front of me now, frantic.

I was covered in blood. I was swimming in blood. I wouldn't let go of him as they slapped Jimmy's face and searched for any sign of life in his half-open eyes.

"Fuck! Get him up here, guys!" Williams screamed. "I've got the bandages out! We've got to do CPR or something! Fuck! Help me get him up!"

JB and Devero pried Jimmy's body from me as I looked on, motionless. I knew it was too late. They lifted as Williams pulled.

I floated in a crimson pool, dazed, noticing beer cans and other contents from our Q boat drifting by. The Q boat had righted itself again drifting about twenty feet ahead, barren and devoid of cargo.

Only when Jimmy's body was resting on the edge of the boat were we able to witness the devastation to his body. At least one of his legs was broken, as well as an arm. His head was distorted and had taken a sickening, unnatural shape.

I glanced up at Williams. I didn't have to say anything. He knew what I was thinking.

He put his head on his knees and clasped his hands behind his neck. He was shaking, overcome by shame, guilt, and loss.

Jim's body lay straddling the side of the boat, his head facing the three of us in the water.

I reached up and closed his eyes.

39

The darkness crept upon us without our acknowledgement, but there was no beauty in this night. These stars, this river, this canyon . . . They had represented such isolated majesty only hours before. Now they represented something else—something ruined, tainted. It was a backstabbing gift that stole from us. A Venus flytrap for our spirits.

We tied the Q boat behind the main one. We moved Jimmy's body into it with as much care as possible, positioning him with as much respect as his crippled, lifeless body would allow. Bandages now covered most of his head, but no amount of bandages could conceal the horrific crime we had committed against god . . . against Jimmy . . . against his wonderful mother.

And while the bandages served no real purpose when applied to a body now completely devoid of any soul or life, we thought they might somehow help us better deal with what had happened.

I guess we hoped that if we couldn't see the depth of the wounds, they somehow might not be real. It was very fucking self-centered, and it was a healthy dose of cosmic justice that it didn't have the desired effect.

After we had placed his body in the boat, I lay there with him for what seemed like an eternity. Over the course of the next few hours, Jimmy's body pretty much bled out. The Q boat became a large plastic bathtub filled with blood.

At some point I jumped up and began beating on his chest in the hope that his god would prove himself to me. I was pounding and screaming so wildly, in such a fit of desperate insanity, with blood flying everywhere, that the others couldn't comprehend any means of consoling me. I was covered head to toe in blood.

At some point, someone came into the boat with me and laid a hand on my shoulder from behind. I had no idea who it was; I just threw my arm back with all of my might, knocking them backward, screaming for them to stay the fuck away from me. If I'd had a gun, there is no question that I would have killed myself right then and there.

I lay down again in the bottom of the boat, completely oblivious to anything or anyone. I held on to Jimmy's tattered, lifeless hand for a good portion of the night.

Now and then, as we would go over a section of the river that jolted the boat, I would taste blood as it splashed over my face. Jimmy's god refused me the energy to wipe it away.

40

There was now exactly zero doubt in my mind that God, if he existed, would spend an eternity seeking vengeance against our souls. God had stripped us of any method of reaching the outside world. His preference was that we suffer. We wouldn't be anywhere close to civilization until tomorrow night.

At some point, Devero began to make an attempt at consoling me. He and JB finally coaxed me out of Jimmy's boat and back into the lead boat. They continued to tell me this wasn't my fault, but I knew that was bullshit. It was. We all had blood on our hands, especially that piece of human excrement, Williams.

As I rose to get into the other boat, streams of my best friend's blood poured down my body, from my hair, from my pockets. I began to scream and cry again. I was in a surreal state of shock—and the sight of this terrified my friends to no end.

I begged Devero and JB to give me the survival knife. I had

every intention of ending it all right then and there. I told them I would cut the line between the two boats, and they wouldn't have to see a thing. I told them we would drift apart and I would go quietly into the night.

They pleaded with me not to make them endure another loss. I finally conceded. How in the fuck would we ever pull it together again?

41

We had no intention of stopping that night. We couldn't. We would go into that dark place in our souls again if we did. We couldn't even allow ourselves to drift for more than a few seconds without beginning to row again, and so after a while, we each took turns. We wanted this river—this darkness, this nightmare of a life—to just *end*.

The passenger boat had not turned over, miraculously. Each of us had a waterproof backpack that contained things such as underwear and weed, with a few boxes of granola bars and a few bottles of water scattered around. There was also a smaller ice chest full of beer, but none of us could even consider drinking beer.

None of us could eat either, but we drank the warm water and smoked a dry carton of cigarettes that we found. The only thing that we really cared about was the key to the van, which had somehow survived throughout the madness. We wanted to once again be comforted by the welcome arms of the conversion van and be off of this godforsaken river.

The flare gun hadn't made it. Even if it had, we had used all of the flares. I doubted that anyone would have seen them anyhow, as we were still deep in the canyon and far away from any structured inhabitance.

So we just pushed and pushed, rowing with fractured ribs and broken fingers, bandages covering our arms and legs. There was no doubt that we all needed medical attention soon.

Every once in a while, we found ourselves staring back at the Q boat. We could still see the shadow of Jimmy's head peeking up from the pool of blood.

The setting was eerie. The walls of the canyon pinned us in, acting as barriers that took from us the ability to at least mentally escape the situation. They demanded that we be *here* and not let out.

Maybe, if there was a god, he struck down the ones he liked so he could make the rest of us suffer. It was clear that he answered some prayers and ignored others. If the intention of this was to teach a lesson, those lessons were taught through inhumane methods. That would make this god a sadist. And that was the only way it made any sense to me.

So here I was, again contemplating the concept of god, albeit no longer as any form of savior.

The night dragged mercilessly on. No one should have to ride in desolation on a raft with their dead best friend in tow. Not if there was a god. The perpetual, guttural anguish was unimaginably difficult. And there was no escape. It was a long, despicable, horrendous night.

Many joints made the rounds, a couple nearly extinguished by tears. I wish I could say they helped. They didn't. They had no effect. We were meant to feel this pain as deeply as it could be felt.

Williams wouldn't even look at me. It was as though he was waiting for me to tell the others that he could have saved Jimmy and didn't. But I couldn't talk about it. The others remained ignorant of the fact that whether Jim had lived or died was actually a decision left up to Williams, and he chose for him to die.

I was too angry to talk about it. I might have lost control. And it was killing me to even be in the same boat as him.

I got up to go sit in the boat with Jimmy again. I felt like I needed to talk to my best friend. For a brief moment I thought that was still an option.

This time, I stopped before I could throw my leg over the edge of his boat. Everything that had occurred in this last unquantifiable period of deep and guttural anguish grabbed me by the throat right then and there, far more than before. And whereas, before, I had collapsed, this time I managed to hold myself upright, frozen.

That was the moment where what had occurred—not just the pain but also the life we'd just stolen from a mother who had already endured *so much* that could never be matched by any amount of devastation . . . A theft unquestionably due to our arrogant attack on the respect of god and nature . . . The repercussions we would all endure . . . The horrific and twisted creation my life had just become—that was when it all hit me.

I stared at him for what felt like hours. I couldn't move. I could feel that it hit the others at the same time, although I was unable to turn and verify this.

Slowly, I began to back up away from Jimmy's boat. I went back to where I had been sitting, and lit another smoke. I stared across the water at what was left of the only person who might have ever been able to save me from myself—that person I had helped destroy through my negligence.

I totally fucking lost it again.

You never understand what death represents until you need to *talk* to the person who died. That's when you realize how final it is. Some people become such a part of us that losing them is like losing a portion of your ability to think and rationalize. I wouldn't be alright until I could hear Jimmy *tell* me I'd be alright—and he'd never again be able to.

A gaping hole in any amount of goodness I thought I might one day be able to achieve had now been formed. We would carry this with us forever. We would never unload this bag.

43

The morning sunlight bled into the sky slowly as the walls of the canyon dipped toward the river. The landscape flattened abruptly.

I had naively thought for hours that if I could just be freed from the walls of the canyon, I might find some form of grace for my mind. I did not. If anything, the walls had served as a barrier, protecting us from what our future held. With the haunting shadows of the canyon that had surrounded us slowly edging behind us, we were now confronted with the full consciousness of all that we would soon have to face. The wide-open terrain seemed far more willing to damn us than the walls of the canyon ever had.

Eventually, we began to make out a shape in the distance of what surely had to be the dock where our journey was to come to an end. We tied up to the rotted wooden edge and climbed out. We all paused in silence as we looked back at the other boat.

I sat down in the middle of the dock and closed my eyes. I was trying to gain enough composure to pick up the phone and make the call I needed to make. I found myself clenching my jaw tightly and pulling my hair—giving God one last opportunity to fix this and prove himself.

God didn't answer. He didn't fix anything. He simply wasn't there.

I knew I now had to make the call that made this all official— that proved it had actually happened and wasn't a nightmare that I would wake from at some point.

I rose from the dock, pulling the rafting company's business card that Jorge had given me from my pack. An English-speaking guy with a Southern accent answered the phone this time. I began to tell him that we had reached our destination. Then I broke down as I tried to tell him what had happened.

He told me that he had a van in the area that could make it to us in twenty minutes and that he would call the authorities for us. I really don't remember anything else until the police arrived, other than occasionally glancing back at the one member of our crew who had not exited the boat, the one who lay half-submerged in a pool of blood at the bottom of a boat tied to the dock.

I remember how cruel the sunlight was. I remember the way that it reflected off of him. But that's all I remember. I don't remember talking to the police, although I somehow convinced them to let me be the one that told Jimmy's mom what had happened. I knew the police told us that his body would be transferred somehow. I don't remember many of the litany of questions that were thrown at us, with the exception of the ones that I didn't want to hear.

"What in the fuck were you guys thinking?"

"Haven't you ever heard of helmets or life jackets?"

"I swear, you fucking kids think you can just come out here and do whatever the fuck you want with zero consequences. You think you can just hop on this river and get fucked-up all day and all night and never pay the price. Was this price high enough? How do you feel about that now? Have you learned your lesson now?"

We got all of the questions that we expected and all of the questions that we deserved. But there was really only one question that stuck with me.

"At what point did you realize that Mr. Smith was deceased?"

Wow. The finality of it. I knew the answer. I would know the answer until the end of time. I just didn't want to put it into words yet. I saw the answer to that question in my mind's eye, playing over and over and over again. I saw it with perfect clarity. My eyes began to well up.

"Take your time, son," the officer said. "I know this isn't easy, but we need to know the details."

There was a long pause as I tried to speak. I could tell that none of my friends had known *how well* I knew this answer until that very moment. I kept replaying the scene in my head, but I just couldn't verbalize it. I couldn't get the first grouping of words out at all. I didn't want to say it because I knew that the moment I did, Devero's and JB's heads would be as fucked-up as mine was. But I had to say it.

"We locked eyes, sir, the moment it happened," I said quietly. "It was just before sundown, yesterday."

JB, Devero, and that piece of shit Williams all looked at me in disbelief. I could see how uncomfortable Williams was in my peripheral vision.

"After we'd gotten separated from the boats, we couldn't . . . we couldn't even *see* each other," I stammered. "The rapids—they came on *so fucking fast*. All I could hear were the screams . . . We'd all been torn to shreds by the rocks and the falls . . . but Jimmy was getting the worst of it. He'd lost his life jacket."

I clenched up, fighting to hold back my tears. "Somehow, fate, karma—I don't fucking know anymore. Whatever it was, it pushed Jimmy and me toward each other as we approached a massive waterfall. He went over a second before me, and he couldn't get his legs in front of him."

I fought to say the words.

"As loud as the rapids were, I still heard the *pop* . . ."

I paused again, trying to make it somehow easier on Devero and JB.

"And his eyes, they were so full of fear but so alive still . . . when I heard that *pop*, there was nothing in them anymore. Nothing. But I still held his gaze . . ."

I closed my eyes as hard as I could and fought the convulsive trembling of my lips.

"His head just . . . Fuck! I'm sorry. It just . . . I can still taste the fucking blood, man. It was just *so awful* . . ." I paused again.

"But that was it, sir," I said, when I could finally speak again. "That was when it happened."

I sat down then on the hard gravel road and put my head between my knees. I couldn't stop thinking about the way the blood had tasted. It wasn't even so much of an issue when I first watched Jim's head collapse in on itself or, in the moments afterward, when I struggled until damn near the point of my own death just to keep some portion of his head, no matter how small, above the surface. I could feel the wound the whole time I was in the river with him. I could feel the unnatural softness of the back of his head. But that wasn't what made me taste it either. It was when I physically saw it. It was when I saw how Jimmy's head had been torn apart in ways impossible to describe. That's when I could taste it. It was an awful thing to remember, tasting blood. But it tasted like copper. It tasted like purgatory.

My friends could see that this was one of the moments that they should have volunteered to do the talking, as opposed to me. But they had no way of knowing what I had been about to say. They didn't know I'd watched his head cave in. They didn't know I'd watched him take his last breath.

And they didn't know, until now, that not only had I watched my best friend endure such unimaginable pain, but some twisted god had chosen my face to be the final snapshot Jim's mind would take before it expired, as his soul was ripped from his body.

But now they knew. And that fucked them up almost as much as it did me.

44

I don't remember anything about the drive back in the van. Not a word was spoken the entire time. The cruel discrimination of the mind only allowed me to remember the most painful moment, when Jimmy's mother opened the door that night.

We had stopped at a gas station about a half hour or so from Jimmy's house so that I could change clothes and wash away the blood that still remained in nearly every crevice of my body. I couldn't let Jim's mom see her son's blood on me.

I looked at myself in the mirror as the last of the orange-tinged water spiraled down the drain. I knew what I was about to do. I remember the way my eyes had looked in the mirror. There was no way anyone could have looked into my eyes and not seen a horrific tragedy hiding behind them.

Having to tell a mother that her only remaining son, the only thing that brought her any joy, this one and only thing she lived for, had been torn from her in the most excruciating manner. Fate could never have been a more cruel and disgusting bastard than it had been to this woman.

That moment would be the first thing I thought of every day and the last thing I thought of every night as I struggled to sleep for the rest of my life.

She knew without my saying a word. She had been through it before. She knew. I can't describe the depth of her pain. It was a level of pain that you don't really know you can get to, but then you get to it. It was so immense. She collapsed to the ground. I pulled her up a bit and put my arms around her. She gripped me as tightly as her muscles would allow, throwing her head back and forth and screaming that it couldn't be true.

But she knew.

Then she grabbed my collar and yanked me toward her, staring into my soul. She pushed me back again and began beating my chest with her fists, cursing me and my friends, and telling me what godless bastards we were. We had caused this.

Our disregard for any rules or morality had extinguished the only glimmer of hope in her life, and she would forever hate us for it. She told me to leave and never come back. She told me not to go to the funeral. She told me that I wasn't welcome there. She said that she would never forgive me and asked that God have mercy on my soul.

He never would, though. Mercy was just a myth.

45

I went home and talked to my parents for hours. I told them everything. They had no lectures for me this time. They knew that this
would be with me forever. They showed grace and understanding.
They talked to me as an adult and tried to console me as such. They
must have seen that the innocence was gone; I would learn from this
without them.

Eventually, I took a shower and climbed into bed. I hadn't talked
to any of the guys. We would talk soon enough. I replayed the accident over and over again in my head, thinking of how it all came on
so fast . . . of the talk Jimmy and I had the night before. Somehow,
on a wet pillow, I finally fell asleep.

When I awoke late the next morning, my mom fixed me a cup
of coffee. She told me that Jimmy's mother had called a couple of
hours earlier and that they had talked for a while. She told my mom
what she had said to me and begged her to help me forgive her.

Me—forgive her.

She wanted me to be a pallbearer at the funeral.

My mom said she'd sounded bad, like she didn't know if she could make it through this. Then my mom came over and put her arms around me, and we cried together.

I met up with JB and Devero at a bar for beers that night. Williams couldn't make it. I didn't care. I hated the guy now. He deserved all of the bad shit that was happening to him.

It was obvious at the bar that we were all still in severe shock. I ranted for so long about how we had been cursed by God that the other guys got irritated. I couldn't help it. There was a fire inside me. I either had to drown it or let it out. It was consuming me.

I was drunk and angry. I went home and called Williams. Shockingly, he actually answered the phone. He tried small talk at first, but I cut through his bullshit right away. I held nothing back and tore into him with voracity.

I could hear him crying as I told him what a piece of shit I thought he was and how I was glad he no longer had any life to fall back on. I told him I was glad that his dad was a piece of shit like him so they could both be ruined together. When I had finished my crude tirade, I told him that I never wanted to see him again after the funeral, and I hung up.

The next day, I wandered aimlessly through my house, sneaking outside from time to time to get high. I was a zombie, dreading the next day when I would bury my best friend.

Jimmy's mom came over late in the day. She let me know that Jimmy had prayed for me every week at church, and she thanked me for being such a good friend. She said that Jimmy had always thought that someday I would do something great—something everyone would be proud of—and he had hoped at that point I would thank God for it. She said that Jim always knew I'd end up finding my way.

I told her that I just wished I could talk to him again. She said I could, that he was listening—and that if I listened really hard, I could hear him answer.

It was obvious that his death had shaken her to the core. But I had no idea that she would care so much about me. That made it hurt so much more.

46

The funeral was disarming in its beauty. I saw the church where the service was held in a way I'd never seen it before. Where once I'd seen a place in which weak-minded congregants gathered to listen to fairy tales, I now saw a building that housed wisdom and respect.

A full gospel choir stood behind the closed casket, all dressed in black robes. Just seeing them sent a chill down my spine. The collective power of their voices forced tears from my eyes. The songs they sang emphasized the sadness of what had happened while still offering hope. The songs resonated with all of those who were present, causing some to weep and others to rise to their feet in praise.

I couldn't believe the number of people who came to pay their respects. I was so proud that Jimmy had affected so many people in his short life. Everyone I spoke with—people I'd never met—told me how much Jim had talked about me, what a good friend I was, the greatness Jim had thought I was capable of. They all let me know they would be praying for me.

After the talk Jim and I had had on the cliff just days before, I almost thought that Jim had set up some big practical joke from the afterlife—all of these people praying for me. Something happened inside me that I can't explain. No matter what the differences in our beliefs were, these people were genuine and good. I was honored that they would pray for me. I knew Jim would laugh his ass off if he'd known I thought that.

I was seated in the first row with the family, between Devero and JB, as people went one by one up to the podium at the front of the church to tell stories about Jimmy and what they would remember most about him.

There was a pause after about the tenth person, and Devero gave me a nudge. I had nothing prepared, but I rose and walked solemnly to the stand. I stood in silence for several seconds, unable to look up at all of these people I'd spoken so poorly of to Jim.

"I didn't prepare anything to say about Jimmy," I began, wiping back a tear. "So please bear with me for a minute. This has been hard . . .

"Please don't take this wrong, but I don't know if there is a god. I can't stand in front of you at a time like this and not be genuine. Jim would want me to be genuine. I fought this battle in my soul too recently, when Jim's father and brother were taken from us. It was so horrible. And now Jim is gone. I'd be lying if I said I weren't fighting it again—now more than ever.

"So, I can't talk about God. I can't talk about his mercy. I haven't experienced it. What I can talk about is Jim. I could talk for days about Jim.

"Jimmy was my best friend in the world. Jimmy was a guy who stood up for what was right. He even stood up for me, a skinny kid with not a lot to offer, every time I couldn't stand up for myself. And Jimmy cared. He cared about all of you—so much that you could never even know. Jimmy cared for his family. He had the strength of character that I could never have . . . He had nothing but forgiveness to offer the man who killed his brother and father. I can't imagine the amount of conviction that must have taken. I can't understand the way the strength of his faith worked to make him such a good man. But Jimmy just wanted everyone to be okay. Jimmy wanted me to be okay. And I haven't been . . . for a while. But he never gave up on me. Never once," I continued, tears now streaming down my face.

"I dreamed that one day I'd have kids, and I'd be able to point to Jimmy and say, 'That's the best role model you could ever want.' And I can't say that now. I can only hope that someday I can get past all of this and become the man that Jim knew I could be.

"Like I said, I'm not like all of you; I can't say that there is a god. But I do know this: If there is a god, Jimmy was his finest creation. And I hope that someday I have the courage to live like Jimmy did. I hope we all do."

I turned and walked toward the casket. I placed my hand on top of it and fell to my knees. I thanked Jimmy for being there for me for as long as he had, and I asked him to never give up on me. My father came and placed his hand on my shoulder.

"Come back to your seat now, Brian," he told me. "You'll make sense of all of this someday. You need to be strong right now."

I hadn't looked up once since walking to the podium. I glanced over at Jimmy's mom as my dad walked me back to my seat. She didn't see me look at her. I don't think she'd looked up the whole time either.

I sat back down in shame, hoping that I hadn't ruined an other-wise beautiful ceremony. I kept hoping that Jimmy's mom would glance over at me and give some nod of approval, but she never did. She spent much of the ceremony in the arms of her loved ones, barely able to stand.

At first, I thought that I might make it past the anger I was feeling because of the love I was being shown on this day, but as the funeral went on, the anger started to push all the love aside.

The weight of the casket that I had to carry didn't scratch the surface of the weight that my now-disposable soul felt in the absence of Jimmy. As I lowered the casket into the ground, saying my last goodbyes to the dearest friend a man could know, that weight began to transform itself into a white-hot anger toward Williams . . . and the hope that he would be more fucked-up than any of us by this.

When it was my turn to offer condolences to what remained of the family, Jimmy's mom cradled the back of my head in her hand, as I had cradled Jimmy's just days before. She just stared at me with tear-filled eyes. She was looking into my soul again.

For a moment, I thought I could see Jimmy in her eyes.

"Brian," she said, "you've got to find yourself, child. That thing in your eyes . . . that pain . . . that anger . . . You've got to get your arms around it. I hope you do, Brian, because it will destroy you from within. It's destroying you now. I see it. You've got to make the choice to see the good things, or your soul will die."

I couldn't say anything. I couldn't tell her that there was nothing good to see.

"I'm so sorry," I said to her. "He was the best person I've ever known."

I looked down at the ground, tears literally dripping from my face, and then I walked away to find a cigarette and a drink. I had to numb the pain.

As I walked toward Devero and JB, I scanned the faces in the crowd, looking for Williams. He hadn't shown up. JB and Devero couldn't understand why he wouldn't be there, but they also didn't know what I knew. They didn't know about the phone call I'd made after we left the bar, either. And while I was glad he wasn't there, I was also pissed that he didn't show.

Fucking coward.

I sat on the front porch chain-smoking at the memorial back at Jimmy's house after the funeral. I probably sat there for two hours, pulling my flask of whiskey out of my coat pocket every few minutes for a swig. JB and Devero sat with me, trying to keep me from going off the deep end. They didn't want to leave me alone.

Jimmy's aunt came out to the porch a short time later and told Devero that he had a phone call. JB and I followed him inside.

OU FRIENDSHIP HATE W
CRISY HEROISM DRUGS IMMO
LICANS SANCTITY LOYALTY CO
INTOLERANCE HIGH TURMOIL D
RITUALITY DISAFFECTED TURBU
MPTION DEATH ACCEPTANCE LUD
ATEFUL FALLING ROCK 'N ROLL
GHTING QUESTIONS ALCOHOL POL
ONVERGING PHILOSOPHY MUSHRO
NREASONABLE LIFE YOUTH ISOLA
OURAGE WEED DEFIANCE EVOLUTI
RSEVERANCE DEPRESSION DELUS
NATURAL SELECTION LAUGHTER
PAIR ORDEAL DETERMINATION D
ADVENTURE IGNORANCE MIND A
ANCE JUDGEMENT UNEASE N
ATED MAGNIFICENT ANGUIS
ITY CONFORMITY PEACE

PART III

A Deficiency of Grace

48

When Devero took the phone at Jim's memorial, we all knew something was very wrong. You could just sense it. Why in the fuck else would someone call a fucking memorial service to talk to someone?

And it was in his face when he hung up. I had the same look on my own face just a few days before. It's the way the eyes lose focus and stare at nothing. It's the way the whole body freezes up. It's the way the jaw hangs not totally open but not closed either. It's the way you can tell that the receptors in the brain have just shut off after hearing a sentence, preventing you from hearing anything after that.

The only thing that he said was "Hello," when he was handed the phone. Then *the look*. After that, he just stood there, paralyzed, for a few moments, with the phone to his ear. And then he set the phone back on the receiver and slowly turned toward JB and me.

"Who the fuck called you at a memorial service?" JB demanded, not noticing the look on Devero's face. "How inconsiderate can people be?"

"Legs, JB, we need to go," Devero told us. "No time for goodbyes."

"Are you friggin' kidding me? I can't just walk out of my best friend's memorial because you got a—" I started to say, but Devero immediately interrupted me.

"Legs! Shut the fuck up! Now! Get in my fucking car! We have to go!" Devero screamed so loudly that heads began to turn, and we left without a single goodbye.

JB had the warped sense to yell, "Shotgun!" right before he hopped in the passenger seat. I sat in the seat behind him in the old blue Honda Accord. Devero hopped behind the wheel.

But we didn't go anywhere. Not yet. Not until he'd told us what happened.

Williams had finally held himself accountable. He had written us a note. I guess it was the only way he could bring himself to tell us how he felt. He wrote that he was sorry that he was such a horrible person, and he was sorry that he had said so many bad things to all of us. He was sorry for being so cruel to so many people for so long. He wrote that he was sorry that he had no courage, not even when he could have saved the life of his friend. He wished he could have had Jimmy's heart, he said.

After he wrote the letter, he set it on the dresser, put on the song "Under the Bridge," by the Red Hot Chili Peppers, and turned the volume up high. Then he sat down on the edge of the bed, put the barrel of a twelve-gauge shotgun in his mouth, and put his brains all over the wall.

Devero said Williams's parents wanted to talk to us to find out what the hell had happened to their son on our trip.

Fuck.

49

We drove to the Williamses' house in absolute disarray. We were all pretty drunk from our individual flasks of assorted cheap liquor by the time we got there. We had also smoked a joint.

None of that mattered, though. You reach a point when the pain can't be subdued or ignored anymore. You reach a point when the numbing agents have no effect. There's no anesthetic strong enough to numb you when your heart is torn out by the claws of karma. It's supposed to hurt, and you're supposed to feel it.

Bleak, man . . . Fucking bleak. This was an atrocious corrosion of the mind and spirit. A week ago, there would have been five of us in a car together. Now there were just three.

Devero was rambling, thinking aloud. "Do we tell them all of the shit he said to Jimmy? Do we take an oath to let that never come out? What about his dad's business shit and the affair? Do we tell them about Williams's meltdown over that shit?"

I wondered whether I should tell the guys about Williams not saving Jimmy when he could have. Williams had mentioned it in his note, but they'd been in such shock that it just didn't register. I wondered whether I should tell them about the drunken call I'd made to him the night before.

I wondered whether he'd planned this all along. Maybe he just wanted one last road trip with the guys before he head-fucked all of us. But I knew I was just making excuses now. I knew it was because of my phone call. If I hadn't called him and said the things I'd said, he wouldn't have blown his brains out.

I wanted to tell them about it all. There was so much that they didn't know. I opened my mouth to speak—to get it all out. To let them know what I knew. But I just couldn't. I was so ashamed. They could see that I was holding back.

"Legs, what's up, man? You okay? You're gonna get through this, man. You're gonna get through it," Devero said, in the most consoling tone he could muster.

I put my feet up onto the seat, legs bent, and buried my face in my knees.

"Guys, I can't fucking do this anymore!" I screamed as loudly as I could. "I wish I were fucking dead! There is no god! *None!* There's nothing out there for me but pain and torture and a fucking miserable, worthless existence! Fuck this, man! He got off easy! Williams got off easy!"

Devero and JB wanted to help. They wanted to keep telling me it would all be fine, but I think they were on the same mental road I was on. Nothing would ever be fine again.

"I wish I had anything worth a shit to say to you," Devero said softly, "but I just don't. Just pull yourself together for a little while longer, man. Put all that pain and anger somewhere else right now. The last thing Williams's family needs right now is to hear you like this. Pull it together, and we'll get fucking plastered after we leave and just drown this shit out for a while—for as long as it takes."

We saw several cars in front of the Williamses' house as we arrived. There was still a police cruiser there, as well as an ambulance. The rest of the half-dozen or so cars must have been family and friends.

In the midst of one of the most beautiful, majestic, and painstakingly manicured landscaping jobs in the city, in front of a home that was no less than an architectural masterpiece, we saw a crouched figure that looked tiny in comparison with its surroundings. It was a man, sitting in the massive garden out front, surrounded by statues, fountains, and exotic plants. He sat with his face buried in his hands, his pants covered in mud. As we pulled closer in the vehicle, we recognized him to be Williams's dad.

He looks so alone, I thought.

I knew that feeling. It was a shitty feeling. I'd felt it way too much in my short life. I felt it now.

We pulled into an open spot in the driveway. His father didn't seem to notice us. We stared quietly for a few moments at the patriarch of this deeply flawed family who was no doubt dealing with his own demons in relation to this and, for a splinter of time, reflected on the horrors of what was about to occur. Then we got out of the car, walked solemnly up the winding path to the door, and rang the doorbell.

Mr. Williams didn't look up once when we walked by him.

50

We were greeted at the door by the last person I wanted to see—a pastor.

I wanted to grab him by his collar, shake him violently, and say, *Pretty awesome god you've got there, pal! You're full of shit! You worship a sadistic puppet master and brainwash your legions of followers to do the same! Then when this shit happens, you say it was somehow part of his plan! That's a pretty fucked-up plan! It's not working out so well lately, so get out of my fucking face!*

I was ready to say exactly that, and I might have done it had Williams's mom not immediately run to me and embraced me so tightly that I almost couldn't breathe.

She was a wreck. She was still in her robe and slippers. Her hair was a mess, and she was slurring from the countless antidepressants and antianxiety medications that she'd no doubt mixed with a heavy helping of vodka.

"Why, Brian?" she tearfully demanded from me. "Why?"

The pastor grabbed her and pulled her close to comfort her as Williams's dad stumbled slowly through the door, never once looking up.

We all gently walked to the living room area. The walls were adorned with millions of dollars' worth of art, which matched the vibrant colors of the seemingly hundreds of Persian rugs. Statues and sculptures stood at every corner and atop every piece of antique furniture.

None of us had really ever felt welcome here. We were rarely allowed near the exquisite couches we were now being asked to take a seat on. We had always been given the vibe that we were beneath these people.

We were each poured drinks made from liquor far more expensive than what our flasks contained, and the small talk about what a tragedy this was soon began.

There were no real introductions made with anyone. I was able to deduce via a moderate bit of small talk that there were two aunts and an uncle in the modest gathering, but that was about it.

While they may have tried to put on a charade about how badly they felt for us losing our friends, it was painfully obvious that they didn't give two shits about us. They wanted to understand the note. Williams's father made that even more apparent when he finally spoke.

"Boys," said Williams's dad, "let's . . . just cut through the bullshit, okay? Tell us what happened with my son and that black boy out there on that river."

Sir, I believe that the 'black boy' you are referring to is Jimmy. Jimmy was my best friend in the world," I said, irritated by the tree from which the apple fell.

"The five of us have been very close for years, sir, but the relationship between your son and Jimmy had become strained lately."

The police officer entered the room now and started to take notes.

"Well, it must have been more than strained, son, don't bullshit me," Mr. Williams shot back. *Condescending prick.*

"Sir," I began again, "with all due respect, I buried my best friend just hours ago. I've had a very tough morning, emotionally. I'm just—"

"*You've* had a tough morning?" he interrupted. "You want to know how I woke up today? I woke up to the sound of my son killing himself, so keep your 'tough day' bullshit to yourself."

There was a dangerous fire in his eyes as he leaned in closer to me.

"Now I want you to tell me what in the fuck happened out there. Stop candy-assing around it."

I was trying to maintain control of the rage that had been building, but I was becoming furious. I was being antagonized by the very same racist asshole that Williams would now never fully become. I tried to regain my composure, but he wouldn't let me.

"I'm talking to you, son! What the fuck happened out there?"

Well, he asked the question . . .

"Sir, your son had become a bigot, just like his father," I said defiantly, "and he spent every day on the river insulting our friend and calling him inferior because he was black."

"Watch your tone with me, son," Mr. Williams sneered angrily.

I glanced around. I'd been too scared and apprehensive about looking in the direction of Williams's bedroom. There was a strand of police tape blocking it off and the door to his room was half-open.

Two things caught my eye that I will never forget. The first thing was the small bit of blood spray that was visible on the section of ceiling and wall that I could see from where I sat. It jarred me. It brought back the night on the river when I had lain completely submerged in Jim's blood. The second thing was what lay at the foot of Williams's bed. It was the rented life jacket, with the burn hole on the chest.

After all of the shit we'd been through, that cheap motherfucker was still concerned with having to pay for the life jacket, so he stuffed it in his backpack to hide it, just like he said he would. He couldn't use it to save a friend who would've done anything for any of us, but he could use it to save a few bucks.

Seeing the life jacket lying there made the rage that had been simmering just below the surface an inevitable eruption now.

"Listen here, son, I don't know what you're doped up on, but you goddamn sure better start giving me some answers. And you'd better show some goddamn respect when you're talking to me."

"I'm not your son," I said. "Stop calling me *son*. I'm my father's son, and my father is a hero to me. You're not. So please don't refer to me as *son*, because by doing so you insult my father just as you and your bigoted son insulted Jimmy."

"Legs, man . . ." Devero said, trying to intercede, but I gave him no chance.

"In addition to hurling ignorant remarks at my best friend for days, what your son did on our final day was unspeakable. I'll tell you because you want to know. Who knows? You might even be proud of him," I said as I rose from my seat in anger.

I glared at the life jacket again and then deadlocked on the pretentious prick.

"You see, we'd all been floating beside our boats on the river on that last day—relaxing, not paying any attention. We were being stupid kids. The falls crept up on us. We couldn't make it back to the boats before we went over them. We went over massive falls, banging into boulder after boulder, but somehow, we all made it through the first few sections alive. You know, I hadn't planned on ever telling anyone this. My two friends sitting here don't even know this. But you want to know what happened. You don't want me to candy-ass it. So I won't.

"You see that life vest over there at the foot of his bed? Look through there. You see it? Your son could've thrown it to Jimmy before we went over the last set of falls. Jimmy was begging him to throw it. I was begging him to throw it. But he wouldn't do it. Your son had pulled himself up into the boat. He was safe. All he had to do was throw the life vest to the one guy who didn't have one, and then we would all still be alive and as unwelcome as ever in your snooty-ass house. But that's not what he did."

"You're telling me," Mr. Williams interrupted, "that my son killed himself because some nigger couldn't swim?"

"I'm telling you that your son killed himself because he was a coward. And seeing as how he learned to be a racist piece of shit from you, my guess is that he learned to be a coward from you as well.

"And another thing," I continued, "if you refer to my best friend that way again, we'll find out with absolute certainty whether you're as much of a coward as your son was."

"You scrawny little son of a bitch, don't you—" he began, but I cut him off.

"Your son also let us in on some other info," I said. "I think you should know this so we have clarity on exactly who's to blame for your son's death. Your son was very upset that you'd swindled a group of investors and cost him his future. He was upset that you lied and stole their money.

"Furthermore, he was embarrassed that you'd chosen to cast aside his mother, your wife, for some overweight bimbo half your age. He said that you spent your investors' money to cover it up. He broke down on one of our last nights there and told us everything. I can't say I blame him for waking you up the way he did this morning."

"He said that?" Mrs. Williams asked, clearly bewildered. One of the aunts began to cry.

"Yes, ma'am, he did," I replied. "He told us everything. He told us that was why he'd been acting the way he had toward all of us, especially Jimmy."

"But, Brian," Mrs. Williams said, "all that happened to his uncle, not my husband. That had nothing to do with us. He must've felt bad for acting poorly and used that as an excuse. It makes no sense . . ." She trailed off vaguely.

I wouldn't have normally bought this story, except that one of the two aunts—the one without her husband, the one crying—wordlessly verified it all. Fuckin' *oops*. Sorry, lady, but your family has *issues*.

But that meant he made it up. *It was all total bullshit.* It made no sense, but it changed nothing. I mean, seriously—*what the fuck?* Sure, I felt bad that I'd just made a complete stranger cry. I hoped that she didn't think she fit into this at all because he'd told us that, but why in the hell would he do that? For the appearance of redemption? *It would only make sense if somehow this were part of the plan all along.*

And if it was part of the plan, and Williams just wanted to off himself anyhow, *why couldn't he just throw Jim the damn life vest?* It had to be because he thought that no one was watching when it all went down. *He was a chickenshit.*

My father used to tell me that it's what you do when people aren't watching that shows who you are. I guess I had always known who Williams really was, but I hadn't wanted to admit it.

He'd always been unhappy. He was always popping pills and doing blow, bitching about how his father belittled him, telling him he didn't deserve what he had, didn't deserve to run the family business. He knew his dad was right: He wasn't capable of running the business—and he wanted to end it before proving him right. He had wanted our sympathy, so he had bullshitted the story. But he wanted to die quickly. He was too chickenshit to risk drowning, even though he was safe. He was too chickenshit to give up the vest. Jimmy fucked up his plan by taking away the sympathy.

But it was still the plan.

"Listen here, you little piece of shit!" Mr. Williams screamed. "How dare you come into my house and speak to me that way? How dare you say those things about my son? Don't try and put this on me—"

I didn't let him get any further. I cut him right the fuck off.

"I'm speaking to you this way in your house because you told us to come over here, and you've been an asshole to us since we got here. Actually, you've been an asshole since we've known you. You disrespected my best friend who just died. I don't give a flying fuck—pardon my language, ladies—if you did any of that shit or not. That just means that in addition to being a coward and a racist, your son was a liar as well. But I didn't raise him; you did. And that's a hell of a legacy you were building there, sir.

"You've been so busy trying to blame someone for your son putting a gun in his mouth that you can't even listen to his own last words. Do you know why he said he didn't have courage in his note? Because you never showed him how to. Do you know why he said he wished he had Jim's heart? Because the one you gave him was shit. He killed Jim; Jim didn't kill him. So stop looking around for who to blame and go look in that fucking antique mirror over there. You'll get your answer."

Everyone was stunned. The cop had stopped writing a while back. I must admit, I was decently surprised as well. Devero and JB sat and stared in shock at what had just transpired. I believe I officially lost the role of *guy who does the talking* at that point.

"So, Mr. Williams, you asked me not to candy-ass things. Did I do okay at it for you, or was I a candy-ass?"

There was zero hesitation in his reply.

"I'll rip your fucking throat out for saying that bullshit in front of my wife on the day her son died! You know where the blame lies! It's on your shoulders! All of you! All of you and that nigger boy you put in the ground today!"

I don't think he was finished talking, but I'm not sure. I'll never get to ask him because of the restraining order. The rage was just so massive; it was just this spinning red madness that overtook my body.

My guess is that I landed somewhere between fifteen and twenty punches on his face before Devero and JB pulled me off of him and the police officer put me in handcuffs.

There was only one good thing that came from that day. Everything else was shit, but one good thing happened. After years of being bullied, tortured, and tormented by those who were stronger and bigger and more powerful—after years of just taking the abuse, being pushed, being punished because I was the little guy—I finally won my first fight.

06/09/06

Socrates famously said that the unexamined life is not worth living. Through the pain of life and all of the turmoil and baggage that comes with trying to understand the logic of it, you have to wonder whether the examined life is worth living as well.

I often think of Jimmy while sitting here in my office, all these years later. I'm thirty-three now. I quit examining life when I was on the river. Maybe that's what's so great about being young: We're not afraid to examine things. We're not afraid to ask the big questions.

Why do we stop? I don't know why. But I decided recently that I wanted to be happy again. It'd been so long. And this is different than simply wishing I were happy. This time I actually want to *be* happy.

So I decided to examine my life. I no longer know whether that's the point of life, though, being happy. Perhaps the reason I've been so jaded, filled with so much anger for such a long time, is that I've been working under the presumption that life is supposed to ultimately be fair. It isn't.

Yet does this mean that we surrender to the unfairness? Should we not seek it out and try to be rid of it? Is our fate predetermined or in our hands? Does this, like religion, have only to do with where we are born?

When you see some chunky celebrity in an infomercial stumping for the hungry foreign kids, it's hard to not remember that life could be far worse for many of us. I'm not referring to chunky person's life; I'm referring to the people whose food they are obviously getting a cut of. My life is better than theirs.

Does fairness for one mean unfairness for another? Must the yin exist in order for us to appreciate the yang? Maybe it does. Maybe we have to submerge ourselves in chicken shit for a while to make the chicken salad.

54

I can't deny that somehow, somewhere along the line, my life got gradually better. I have a great wife now. I have awesome kids that mean the world to me. And I'm their hero.

Seriously. Me. A fucking hero. That blows my mind. If God exists, why would he play such a cruel joke on these children? Why give them me as a hero?

And they're such great kids. My only goal in life is to not let them be like me—which is hard, because they want to be just like me. If only they knew . . .

They make me smile, though. They make me grow. They make me a better man. I can't handle the thought of ever letting them down.

When you look at Nietzsche and his philosophical dwellings, you might think the guy had some things figured out. Nietzsche disliked the religious community because he felt that *extrinsic* motivation was wrong—that if the reason for being good was to get a prize at the end—Heaven—you had a bad moral compass. However, if the reason for being good was so that your kids might also be good, this kind of *intrinsic* motivation would seemingly be proper.

But Nietzsche was operating under a possibly false pretense: that the only reason most people believed in God was to get into Heaven. Not all people who believe in God are in it for the gift bag at the end of the party.

So fuck Nietzsche.

And Galileo, man—that guy had some things figured out. He said, "I do not feel obliged to believe that the same god who has endowed us with sense, reason, and intellect has intended us to forgo their use."

So, believing in God doesn't necessarily make someone an idiot. Being an idiot is independent of religion. But if there's a god, Galileo and I believe he'd prefer we acknowledge what is apparent and not act like dipshits.

I'm pretty sure that's the point Jim was trying to make to me all along.

I took over my dad's real estate business a few years back, and I make really good money now. But I've been coasting for years. I feel as though I haven't progressed an ounce mentally since those days. And I need to. I need to for my wife. I need to for my kids. I need to for myself.

But my mind has been stuck on the river. Perhaps the downward spiral my spiritual life took crippled me long ago. I can't help but think that religion has destroyed so much . . .Yet my mind and my life, in its absence, seem also destroyed. The feeling that it can't be true and the guilt of not believing in it have been at war with each other.

How do I reconcile? It's so hard in these times to find someone who appears intellectually above the status of an inbred goat who can actually make an argument for spirituality. And saying that, I feel the guilt, because I once knew someone who was at the same time both spiritual and genius . . . Jim.

This leads me to the knowledge that part of this reconciliation of the soul must include not looking down on those who are spiritual. I realized that at Jim's funeral for the first time, but I made the choice to file it away somewhere and ignore it. I should've made a better choice.

And not bitch-slapping the mentally deficient religious zealots can be hard. Just ask Galileo.

Jimmy used to quote Bible verses to me. He didn't quote them like a tearful Jimmy Swaggart, who had just thrown the bone at an exotic dancer, nor in the manner of Jim Bakker, who had stolen money from the poor. He quoted verses because he was genuinely good and wanted to help people. He saw the wisdom in the words, and looked past the hypocrisy of those who twisted them. Jimmy never said, "This is 100 percent factual history." He said, "This is a good way to live."

And I know what you're thinking right now: *Please tell me this guy isn't about to start preaching.* I'm not. But the reason that you're thinking that may be because you've done what I've done for so long—operated under the assumption that if idiots perform acts of lunacy while quoting from a book of religion, then the book they are quoting from must also be lunacy. There's a shitload of lunacy in books of religion, but what I've ignored entirely is that there's a little bit of wisdom in there as well, and it's not exactly rocket science to distinguish between the two.

When I think of the verses Jim used to say to me over and over again, I realize that he had found the wisdom. One verse that he quoted me was Matthew 7: 21–23, which said, "Not everyone who says to me, 'Lord, Lord,' will enter the kingdom of heaven, but only he who does the will of my Father who is in heaven. Many will say to me on that day, 'Lord, Lord, did we not prophesy in your name, and in your name drive out demons and perform many miracles?' Then I will tell them plainly, 'I never knew you. Away from me, you evildoers!'"

That verse always got me. It gets me still today. And I must say, when I hear the term *evildoers*, I can't help but think of many on the religious right inventing bad guys and scaring us into voting for them. Politics has left an ugly stain on the Bible lately. Bigotry has found solace in its arms. I wish I could talk with Jim about it.

But as I catch myself looking down my nose at those who start wars and look away from famine in the name of god, I know that their god is not the one Jim believed in. Their god is printed and passed for merchandise. They could never be allowed in the place Jim hopefully now resides.

And sadly, their imminent demise is what somehow strengthens any faint light of spirituality still yearning to shine in my heart. That can't be good either.

It's like the Williams family. They said they were Christians. They bashed anyone who believed differently from how they did. They never gave a nickel or a drop of sweat to help anyone other than themselves. And, somehow, they figured they were shoo-ins for a kick-ass afterlife.

It's the Williams families across the globe who make me want no part of their "faith." But I'm pretty certain that, if there is a god, and Williams went to give him the ol' *Hey, bro, I'm here! Let's party!* then that god would say, *I have no friggin' clue who you are. Get the hell out before I call the cops. And tell your pops he's out also.*

Another verse that Jimmy would throw at me while manning a bong at five in the morning as the sun was just about to blast across our little piece of the hemisphere was something from II Corinthians.

I don't want to sound like a Republican here by quoting another verse, because I no longer associate myself with them—and there's no need to get into that now, because it would take many more chapters to explain how hard they suck, cloaking themselves in the Bible while ignoring everything in it . . . But here's what this one was about:

There was this guy named Paul. Paul was pretty pissed off, apparently. And it wasn't because he was given such a lame and common name, when other guys got cool and original names like Moses or Noah. No, Paul was pissed off because he had some kind of serious physical ailment. It was never described very thoroughly, I guess, but it was stated in Acts that he was pretty much blind . . . although this has been a subject of much debate.

And who is one of Paul's wingmen? Jesus. Yes, *that* Jesus. Jesus H. Christ. The same Jesus that went town to town healing people and raising them from the dead. Paul spent almost all of his days stumping for his buddy Jesus. The whole time he's doing this, he's praying that his own ailment will be healed. And every morning, he'd wake up and say, *Son of a bitch, man. Not cool. I still can't see shit.*

(I'm paraphrasing here, by the way.)

Anyhow, one day, Paul prays to his buddy Jesus and says, *Hey, bro, I'm not sure if you noticed, but I have this serious undisclosed ailment that's really becoming a pain in the ass. And every day of your entire life, you're pulling this Dr. Jesus stuff—fixing people left and right. You fixed that Lazarus dude, and he was, like, dead. Are you ever gonna hook a brother up?*

And do you know what Jesus said back to Paul?

"My grace is sufficient for you, for my power is made perfect in weakness."

That's the verse that always brings me back to the river, to the night Jim and I had our talk on the cliff.

I always wanted to bitch about everything that was wrong. I always assumed that there couldn't possibly be a god who would allow a kid to be six feet tall and weigh a hundred and seventeen pounds. I always assumed there couldn't possibly be a god who would allow skinny little shits like me to get their asses kicked by football players and bullies every single week. I always assumed there couldn't possibly be a god who would allow a person as truly good as Jim to die such an awful and painful death, or allow a saint of a woman like Jim's mom to lose her entire family. And you know what? Maybe there's not. But I do know that there's beauty that exists when you look for it, and I know that the grace that I've been shown is sufficient.

That's what I think of when I look into the eyes of my children. I was kicked in the balls by life so hard for so long, but if that was the pain I had to endure so that I could get to the point that I actually had something so beautiful and perfect to live for, then the smallest amount of grace that I had been shown was sufficient.

So, is that evidence of a Higher Power? No, it's not. But I'm training myself not to look for the evidence now. I've got to look for the beauty.

Could it be that we are all just a random occurrence? Yes, it could. Could random occurrences be so profound? It is possible. Could it all have just *happened*? Yeah, it could have. But I really just don't know anymore.

You see, the science part of it is easy. Perhaps it's ironically the path of least resistance to take the *intellectual* route. Science can't see what I see and feel when I look at my kids.

And I guess that's where this all leaves me. As much as I may accept the lack of logic that might suggest a Creator, I cannot deny that a Creator may be the only logical explanation for the innocence and beauty we all possess so early on. Try as it might, science cannot explain the smile of a child. It cannot explain true friendship. It cannot explain the desire of one man to save the soul of another. It cannot explain the height of emotion I had when the sunlight burst through the canyon for just a blink in time so long ago on that river nor the depth of anguish that followed as the sunlight passed. No matter the vast number of experiments performed, science will never tell us what is in this composition of the spiritual soul that tells us to pick ourselves up again, to bounce back.

I just know now that I must. And it is that lack of provable explanation that, oddly, gives me comfort in this. My father, Jim, and now my children have all captured my spirit. They have shown me that when the flag falls, you must gather the strength and conviction we all possess inside to grab it and march it further up the hill—if for no other reason than knowing that the alternative is submission to a fate that we may or may not control.

No matter what dies inside me as that which is around me succumbs to harsh ends, something inside me has always told me to keep going. I don't know what it is that keeps pushing me, but I think I'm okay with that now. I'm okay with not knowing what it is, with not giving it a name.

Maybe someday science will explain it, and I'll have to reconcile again. Or maybe it's the grief, the loss, the pain. Maybe it's the guilt that makes me *want* it, *want* God to exist. And whether or not that is weakness or false hope, I don't really give a shit. I just think now that *something* might be there.

Something.

And that may be enough.

ABOUT THE AUTHOR

Matthew S. Hiley is a novelist from Fort Worth, Texas. He is happily married to his college sweetheart and a proud father of four children. A terrible musician, a reprehensible fisherman, and a mediocre golfer, Hiley decided to take a break from the business world a couple of years ago to pursue his lifelong passion of writing. His writing style is sharp, witty, and unafraid.

AUTHOR Q & A

Q : What inspired you to write *Hubris Falls*? What are some of the books that may have influenced your story and style of writing?

A : Like a lot of folks, I was a moron in my youth. I may still be one. I actually took a rafting trip along this route when I was nineteen, and it was incredibly beautiful and scary. I always wanted to write a story about how smart we think we are, how naïve we actually are, and how invincible we feel at that age.

My favorite book of all time is Catcher in the Rye. I felt I had a real connection with Holden. I even named my son after him. I also enjoyed greatly the madness of Hunter S. Thompson and the originality of Kurt Vonnegut. They've always been the benchmark for me.

Q : How long did it take you to write *Hubris Falls?* What is your writing process like? Do you have any unique writing habits?

A : I originally wrote Hubris Falls in college as a twenty-page short story. The professor liked it so much she had me read it in front of the class. The story always seemed to connect with people. I held on to that story, always wanting to make a full-length novel out of it. It took about a dozen years, but I finally threw together a first draft in 2006. I worked on it on and off for a few more years, then self-published a version in 2010. I always wanted to do it better, though, so I dug in with my publisher, Greenleaf, and I think I finally made the version I'd always wanted. It's been several years in the making.

My writing process generally consists of writing a short description of the story I want to tell, then writing an outline for it. After that, I try and flesh out my characters, making a list and describing them in depth. And then I just write. I try and dedicate a set amount of time each day and just wrap my head inside a different world.

Q : What were some of your favorite chapters to write in *Hubris Falls* and why? On the other hand, were there any parts of the story that were particularly challenging to write? If so, what about those sections were challenging?

A : My favorite chapters to write were probably the chapters that took place in the van on the way to the river, with the stop at the Waffle House. The freedom of the open road is something I have a great fondness for. That time in our lives when we just hopped in cars and drove countless hours somewhere with our friends . . . it doesn't get much better than that.

Q : The themes of race and bullying play a large role in the novel. Can you talk a bit about how these themes played out in the story?

A : A lot of things that happened in this novel actually occurred in real life. I was the kid that was always incredibly skinny, and I was an easy target for bullies. People often don't remember how difficult it can be to be a teenager sometimes, especially when you're not physically perfect. Kids can be mean as hell. Bullies are garbage. I wanted to offer redemption at times for the kid getting knocked around but also remain realistic about it. Bullies don't go away. You'll meet them all through life. We have to learn to stand up to them. As for race . . . I've always had a pretty diverse group of friends. Growing up in any part of America, you'll see racism if your eyes are open. What plays out in the story is a real relationship between two kids of different races and the way in which we notice that there are varying degrees and varying faces of racism . . . it's not always a Klan member or a Nazi. Sometimes you find out it's your friends.

Q : Jim and Brian have many conversations about religion and spir- ituality. What motivated you to have this as a key part in their rela- tionship? What do you think of the discussions they had?

A : The spiritual journey in Hubris Falls was exactly my own . . . I went to all of the different schools, churches, and church camps I wrote about. I was the kid that got "saved" every year, until someone finally told me that once was enough. I studied religion a good bit in my younger days and even more when I began to turn away from it. And I love to argue. I genuinely enjoyed arguing about religion in my college days, especially with religious folks. Many of my friends and I would sit around drinking, smoking weed, and debating religion, philosophy, politics . . . I think being able to have conversations with people you disagree with is important. And I also believe, from those conversations, that genuinely good and intelligent people are on both sides of the debate.

Q: Do you have a favorite character in the story? If so, what about that character appealed to you?

A: My favorite character in the book has got to be Jimmy. He's based on my roommate in college, one of my closest friends. I like the fact that he's very different in most of his views than his close friends and never fails to stand up for them. He's been through a lot but still finds the time to genuinely watch out for his friends.

Q: Do you think that Williams was a redeemable character? Do you think he could have resolved his issues with Brian and Jim if they had all lived?

A: I'm not sure Williams would ever take a shot at redemption. Everyone knows the fun asshole in our younger years. I think most intelligent folks begin to move away from them when they begin to realize that it's not a character they're playing . . . they're actually just assholes, and that's typically rooted in deep unhappiness. I don't think Williams would've ever genuinely admitted any fault concerning his views on Jimmy and race.

Q : Do you think any of the characters were particularly at fault for either Jim's or Williams's deaths? If so who and why?

A : Williams played the largest role in Jimmy's death by not throwing him his life jacket, but everyone's collective lack of adherence to basic safety played an almost equal role.

Q : What inspired you to include drug and alcohol use in the novel? What do you think the drug usage says about the characters and how did it influence the story?

A : I included the drug and alcohol use, just like the language, to try and keep the story as real as possible. I'm not saying that all college kids party like this, but many of them do. I don't feel that recreational drug use says anything negative about the characters. This is set at a time in life when people get a little crazy. Kids want to get extremely wasted sometimes, and sometimes that has consequences.

Q : Do you have another book in the works? If so, can you share a bit about its plot?

A : I'm currently working on Book 2 of my Baseball Dads trilogy. The first in the series followed Dwayne Devero as he has a complete mental breakdown while trying to deal with keeping his financial head above water while keeping up with high society and children's baseball. Dwayne becomes a vigilante serial killer while coaching his son's team to the championship, and after burying a decent number of local assholes under the bases at the local ballpark, he goes into hiding. Book 2 will focus on Dwayne coming out of hiding to become an undercover killer for the FBI and run for congress . . . while coaching his son's baseball team all the way to the Little League World Series.

QUESTIONS FOR DISCUSSION

What are some of the major themes in *Hubris Falls*? Discuss how these themes play out in the story (e.g., religion and spirituality, race, drug abuse, politics, bullying).

The location and scenery of *Hubris Falls*, such as the cave and the towering canyon walls, play a large roll in the story. Discuss how the setting helps develop the story and the characters.

Discuss the troubled nature of Williams. Williams himself did not believe that he was a redeemable figure at the end of the novel. Do you agree? What could Williams have done either before or after Jim's death to redeem himself?

Jim and Brian discuss the topic of religion throughout the novel. Do you think Brian would have returned to Christianity had Jim survived, or would Brian have continued down the path he was on?

Jim is presented as a tragic character. What are some of the aspects of Jim, both good and bad, that led him to be seen this way? Had he not died, would he still be considered a tragic character?

In the final chapters Brian reveals that he has been plagued with guilt ever since the events at the end of the trip. Do you think he is being too hard on himself and it is time to forgive, or is his guilt well founded?

The discussions of race are centered around Jim and mainly between him and Williams; however, Devero says little in these discussions while also being of minority descent. Do you think he had views on this topic that were not expressed? If so, what do you think they were, and should he have spoken up?

Brian gives Mr. Williams a beating at the end of the novel. Did Brian go too far given the situation and the tragedy Mr. Williams woke up to, or did Mr. Williams deserve those punches from Brian?

Had Williams and Jim both lived, do you think they would have been able to reconcile? Would they be able to remain friends?

If Williams had not committed suicide, do you think he could have reconciled with Brian, or do you think their relationship was beyond repair?

There are some disturbing depictions of bullying in the novel, such as the naked photos taken of Williams while he slept. What trauma might this have caused Williams when he saw the photos? Do you think this bullying played a role in his decision to commit suicide?

Most of this story takes place in the summer of 1997. How do you think the conversations of race, politics, and religion might have changed if they had taken place today?

JB and Devero were less dynamic characters than Brian. But, having gone though many of the same experiences as Brian, do you think JB and Devero underwent the same coming-of-age journey? Are there any places in the story that show this?

The use of drugs and alcohol is constant throughout the novel. How did their usage affect the characters and the story?